C. Ramsay

The God Seed

And

The Dalai Lama's Wife

STEREO A TYPICAL PRESS

STEREO-A-TYPICAL PRESS
Denver, Colorado
Stereoatypicalpress.com

First printing November 2016

ISBN 9781946293008

Printed in the United States of America

PUBLISHER'S NOTE
This is a work of fiction. Names, characters, places, and incidents either are the product of the author's imagination or are used fictitiously, and any resemblance to actual persons, living or dead, events, or locales is entirely coincidental.

*

Once upon a time, in a land by a sea, there was born a small child.

And this child was, as all children are, a perfect seed of God potential.

Now this seed of Godness that lay inside this boy – for it was a boy child but could easily have been a girl child for all beings have inside them the God Seed – was not of a Godness that resembled anything like what you might have come to think of God to be. It did not resemble anything in any human form either. The God of which this was a seed was much more like an energy force. This God is, well, a little like the indescribable effervescence that connects all people to each other and perhaps too is the record of all that has come before, beating and thumping out the rhythm of one life; one organism pulsing. Not the God of creation nor the God so much, of omnipotence, but the God that is one with all things, that does not know separation, that has become energy. A bit hard to describe in words really but perhaps you'll recognize it better as the story of this journey – that of an unusual, and in all ways, obscure, Woman – does unfold.

He, this boy, had inside him, as all people do, this potential, this *access* to the energy, the *access* to the opportunity to be one with it, and to, by accessing it and knowing unity, experience all that has ever been experienced.

It was a powerful seed that way.

With its maturity would come the ability to know by the first hand and in the deepest way, all human suffering and all human beauty, such is its power.

He would, were he to manifest this potential that he and all others possess to access this energy, experience all this knowing in no more time than could be fit through the eye of a needle or could sit upon its tip. Instantaneous would be the speed of all this knowing.

Now, as this child grew through the years, many things happened to him, much that was bad, some that was good, and he grew very involved and entwined into the details of each of these many happenings. With each iteration, each occurrence, he became more and more involved. Each time, he focused more of his energy on the specifics, the details. In this way, he grew to believe the details important.

As he grew further, he became enmeshed in knowing the culture in which these details took place, and he grew to believe that the culture mattered too. He did the same with each of many, many categories which could be said to be specific to himself and to the particulars of the way in which the things that happened in his life, good and bad, happened to him, the ways in which they were experienced by him – things like religion, gender, sexual orientation, height, weight, and his list went on and on and he told himself that each of these, these too were important.

And so he turned in directions far from his God Seed inside of him. All the while that his focus was being misdirected though, experience was still unfolding, time was still going on and action was still required. In this way, action misdirected became habit formed. Those habits took hold, became meaningful to the boy…

…and the habits grew.

The seed of this God potential remained in him as he aged, but its person, the boy, was too much in the world for the Seed to grow or manifest. Soon concern, anxiety, competition, fear and an uncertainty of confidence drew much dirt and detritus, debris and weight to join with misdirection and habit and encircle the God Seed inside the boy.

This continued for many years until the boy around the seed was a grown man and even after.

The Man around the Seed began to think himself enclosed, a complete whole unconnected elsewhere. He began to forget, to forget all that he had known when first he'd arrived and in earliest childhood.

In this forgetting, he began to think that he was a single being, discrete, separated and unconnected to the other beings like him. Alone like this and floating unconnected, his mind became fooled. The body he and each of them had, lent itself to this fooling, this misunderstanding, this *illusion*. And because of this illusion created by the bodies – of discrete, solitary wholeness – there comes a time into each life when the people forget that it is other than that. They forget that they are connected to each other by limbs as strong and as real as that which connects shoulder to wrist, hip to ankle.

This feeling, this feeling of separateness, added to the anxiety of the God Seed being. It added to his fear, his uncertainty. Those things in turn, like the concern and competition before them, they attracted still more negativity around the God Seed.

The weight of the body surrounding the Seed, the heavy feeling of it, grew, with the weight of the negativity and debris until finally, though the man remained thin, the heaviness of the soul weighed down on him until he felt that a deep, deep well surrounded the Seed of God Potential, a well which seemed much of the time to be lined with layer upon layer of hardest brick. This was a weight, a feeling, a well, which drew all energy away from the Seed.

Now, it is at just this exact point in the life of each of these beings that often, usually, almost always, the Seed of God

Potential would wither. Wither clean away and die, it would, most times.

In this one however, in *this* man, this one particular man, a man who had been, once, a child, while it did not grow, his Seed of God Potential did not wither and die either. His seed, for whatever reason, alternately slumbered and struggled on, there inside him, instead of either growing or, like most, dying.

The weight of the debris around this God Seed though, *did* grow. It grew till the God Seed thought itself inside that well, and the man, he thought it too. He grew distant from the Seed. He thought instead, about the well. A deep, deep well, he thought himself in, enclosed and claustrophobic. Fifty feet and more was this dark and narrow well, and surrounded on all sides by dense banks of fog. Lined with hardest brick at times, the man's well was, and the bricks, they gave off dust which choked at the throat of the man. At other times, the brick lining the well was crumbling and molding, and it gave off spores and odors which gagged and sickened the man. Cold and damp was the well, and inside it, was the man, hungry and sad and alone.

The man who was the God Seed because unlike most, his Seed had not withered and died, he kept his feet moving inside this well all the while. Lashing about with the whole of his legs, kicking, cycling, moving, never stopping. All the time, as

She watched, he moved them, treading water inside the weightiness that felt like a well around him. He did this odd thing because toward the bottom of this well appeared bracken water. The brackishness, or the water, or both, they threatened all the while, to consume him.

*

On a cliff, overlooking the Pacific, The Woman, She closed the door behind Her and with only a small pack of nuts and water upon Her back, walked with unhurried pace away from what had, for a few years, been Her home. The direction in which She walked was toward the sun's rising.

Though a small dwelling, it had been the right size to house Her; not too large and not too cramped. She was at peace there, with a wall to the west made only of glass where She had watched every day, the effluvious array of color released as the sinking of the sun into the sea caused sea and sun to merge – two sources, one life.

And too, though the walls inside were bare, She carried not book nor photo, knickknack nor painting away with Her upon her back. The walls had been bare the whole time, throughout the duration of Her stay and were not bare now simply because of Her departure, for it was inside of Her that was as decorated as the finest gallery and richest garden, was inside of Herself She carried the decorations of Her life and not outside Herself at all.

And, *that* Woman, her door closed, She began to walk.

*

The God Seed, he kept on like that, treading bracken water inside thick, weighty, sooty, lung-choking dust. And, many years later, having gotten the hang of keeping the weightiness and the brackishness and the choking dust from consuming him, and having gotten the hang of keeping always in motion, well it was from this vantage point and while in the grip of that constant motion, that the man in which the God Seed still dwelled with its light that was a beacon if not for the dirt that hid it, the God Seed hoping for the chance to become real and shed itself of the muck that doused it, fell in love.

*

It was, oddly, through his nose that first he became aware of The Woman near him. It was a smell that he would describe as beautiful, but he thought, perhaps it was only to him that the scent brought memories of beauty, and in this way caused him to think it beautiful.

This he thought because the smell itself was really one more of earth and ancient processes. Not one of compost but still one of becoming – of leaves becoming detritus becoming soil becoming food becoming life.

*

Now The Woman with whom he fell in love, and who had walked from the sea, She had a garden around her God Seed.

It was from this garden that the smell arose – the ancient and beautiful smell that spoke of loam and wood and richness and connection to the man. So organic, this smell, that it was a part of him, a part of the most ancient form of him, from the very moment that first he breathed it in.

So much so, that he wanted to be near that smell, and near its source.

The man, he breathed in deeply of it whenever he could, whenever She was near, perhaps wanting too, the energy that had created it.

Yes, the energy that had created it, he could feel the pull inside himself, toward that. But he did not know what it was that pulled him and thought instead that it was a pull of a different kind which he experienced. For though he could sense and even smell the garden and the God Seed in The Woman, a seed which *had* manifested, he could not yet *know* that he sensed it, not yet know what it was.

*

For this, being allowed to be near this aroma, to breathe it in, and for the life it created in him, he was profoundly grateful.

For a while.

Until he forgot.

He forgot to be grateful and became instead, jealous.

He forgot this because the material of his love was not made of the material of her love. He had wanted things for himself – energy, life, richness – the things of her garden that she had created, and so he had called these wants of his, love.

And so, in calling his wants love, he could not hold onto his gratefulness or the profundity of it.

He forgot.

And in his forgetting to be grateful, he grew jealous.

He grew jealous of The Woman, and of her garden.

*

Now because of Her garden, The Woman walking from the wall of windows in the west, The Woman with whom the fighting, churning man fell in love, could both see the God Seed that dwelt in the man and She could know what it was.

Once, long ago, this had happened to Her. Lifetimes ago, it had been Her who had been recognized. The God Seed inside Her had been recognized, and by one who also had known what it was in Her that called out to him to be remembered.

This one who remembered Her, he had been an archbishop of the people, well known the world over and he had stopped a moment beside The Woman, who was but a girl then, and he, who had gone then by the name of Tutu, had recognized Her. The Woman liked that, the not being alone anymore, She liked being near someone else who also had a garden. She had, at that time though, not known that it was quite within the realm of the possible that She might never experience again that recognition, might never share again, with another garden-decorated God Seed. For at that time, She was young, a child, and thought still that everyone had accessed their garden, and even the path beyond it. She had thought still that everyone could recognize these, and know too what they were recognizing. She thought back then, that this would happen to Her many, many times. Though many had stopped beside Her since, called like the man by the type of energy that encircled Her garden, not one yet since that archbishop, had known what it was that had called them to Her.

*

And yet, despite Her Loneliness, Her own desire for a manifested God Seed, for another soul with a garden around *it*, with which to share, despite this, She kept on.

Despite this big L Loneliness, that was not a longing for other people, but was a kind of Loneliness for another soul of a particular type, The Woman walked.

She walked
    and She walked
        and She walked.

*

And because She walked, She came, eventually, upon the man.

She came upon the man who was inside a well inside of fog.

She knew, coming upon him that he held within him an unwithered God Seed.

The Woman also knew, having recognized his God Seed, that it was very rare that the man had not yet at this late stage, lost his God Seed – that it had not withered under the weight of all the debris, the cultural detritus, which had been attracted to it and which surrounded it. She saw all this and loved this about the man, that something had kept his God Seed alive.

And so, for a time, beside this man, She stayed. She lingered near.

But Her love for the man was of a different variety. It was a love of the kind She had for all beings and so Her love was created from a different source and was built up with vastly different materials from that love which was felt by the man around the God Seed, who was a well every bit as much as the well that surrounded him was him – both body and soul.

For yes, She could see the well. She could see the well as clearly as She could see his God Seed not yet withered. She

could see the thick fog surrounding his well and separating
him.

It was because Her love was of a different variety and
material that She could see the well and not just the God Seed.
And it was because of Her Garden that her love was of the
kind She had for all beings and was built up of these different,
stronger materials.

Because of these things She could, unlike the man, see
both his well and his God Seed clearly.

Very clearly.

With greatest Clarity.

And, because She saw it clearly, what *She* saw when *She*
looked out at the churning, fighting, moving man was, well,
She could see that his well was, in actuality, only three feet
deep.

And too, it was dry.

It was a dry well, for it held no bracken water, no water at
all.

The man, he could step down at any time.

Hers was the burden to see this.

How deep for Her the burden of the shallow well.

*

The Man, he could stop his feet from moving and be still, for he was safe. He could set his foot, either one, right up over onto dry land and stand up. He could even step straight up out of the well – which was, in truth, only his own body and soul, which both held but also hid the God Seed inside of him.

In stillness, he could be with The Woman then, in The Happiness For What Is, that had created the garden in which She played.

For this, The Happiness For What Is, is what had created the garden that surrounded Her and then had allowed it to grow.

And it was because of this Happiness, that She was happy and wanted for nothing at all unless it was for someone with whom to share Her garden, someone who too, could see the garden around their own God Seed.

For that however, She would need to meet someone in whom the God Seed of Potential to Become Real had not only not-yet-withered, but had also grown. And *that* had proven rare beyond even the wildest of Her wild imaginings of what was possible in this Earthen world.

At first, The Woman knew not what to do at such a predicament – having found a non-withered God Seed of Potential.

Such a predicament, thought She – having found this Seed beneath such enormous weight and in one feeling discrete and unconnected and as if swimming in deepest ocean inside a narrow, nasty enclosure.

It seemed only sensible to The Woman that She would tell the man of the truth of his situation.

Then, knowing, he would simply stop his feet from kicking. He would take the single, simple step up and out and join Her beyond the tiny, restrictive, suffocating little well. And they could be together in the garden. Or, on the path beyond the garden.

Now She had noticed too, that, *occasionally*, the man would peek out, sideways, out from his eyes. Other times it was straight down at the ground that was right in front of him. She did not know what this was *exactly*, but She did recognize for certain that it was a time when he was, of a moment, somewhat slightly different from the other times.

And so, when She determined She would speak to the man of his situation, it was one of these brief moments of what seemed to Her to be a glimmer of recognition of Truth in him, which She chose for Herself. It was in one of these glimmering moments that She chose to speak to him about Truth.

So, She waited.

*

And then, a year passed, another of those moments occurred. In She leaned, when the time was right, close to him, that he could hear Her, and smell Her and feel the beating of Her heart that was the same as the beating of his heart.

In She leaned...

... and She told him.

She told him of the well.

Gently, ever so gently, She spoke.

At times, She would whisper on the wind.

It will all be alright, She whispered into that wind, that it might take Her words, their *feeling,* to the God Seed.

Of the dryness in the well, She told him.

Of the land just beside him, She spoke.

It is only three feet deep, this well of yours, She said.

In truth, She described to him, *it isn't actually a well at all but only your own self – the weightiness you carry, the debris which covers the God Seed of Potential which you also carry within you.*

Let It Go,

She told the man.

Let It Go, this weighty debris, and you will stand up, straight and tall, beside the well. In one fell step, easy as that, your God Seed will be free and you as well.

But, The Woman had already gotten too close, too close to the man, and she got kicked by the feet of the man which were never still.

*

The Woman went away a little then. But only a little, and She came back and lingered near the man who because of the God Seed had the Potential to Become Real. She came back a little less than She had before, and came in a little less close then She had, and She waited.

She waited for another of the special moments, the moments in which it seemed to Her, that perhaps he was experiencing a moment that held inside of it for him, a glimmer of Truth – the merest reflection of Truth.

And then, two years passed, another of the moments occurred.

And The Woman tried again.

She leaned in, close to him that he could hear and feel Her, but not *as* close.

Gently, She nurtured the man. Of the well and of its dryness, of its true height and origins, of his nearness to the land, She spoke. Boldly, She told him of the garden that awaited him, encouraging him to Let It Go, to let go of his well.

It is not of darkness your heart whispers to you, but only of the unknown, The Woman said to the God Seed. *The unknown is a thing so hugely, vastly different from the thing that darkness is.* As different, She could have added, as is an ocean from a well.

But, still, The Woman and Her words, they were much too close. Still The Woman got kicked out at by the frantic, lashing feet of the man, the feet that were never still.

Again, She was forced to move a ways away from the man, for Her own protection.

*

This happened many times.

Each time, The Woman was forced to come back a little less, to move in a little less close than the time before.

*

Now the man, while he was in the well, he wasn't just moving. He also held fast to four roots and branches. He had one in each hand but that left two needing to be held, as hard as that was, by the toes of each foot, each *moving* foot.

This was hard for the man. It was very, *very* hard.

BUT, it was familiar.

So, on he held though letting them go would have been easier.

Even in its discomfort, it was a discomfort he knew.

So he held on.

These roots, this familiarity, they helped him to survive, so She could not, She knew, tell him that they also kept him from living, from thriving.

*

On the fourth of her attempts inward toward him but less-close than the one before, She tried *not* speaking. She tried just reaching straight in. She thought to simply hoist the man directly out, it was only three feet for goodness' sake.

But, that time, She got kicked *and* bitten.

*

On the fifth of Her attempts, and the second non-speaking, She thought to help him out in sort of a sideways kind of a way, a sort of *peripheral* way. Show him the garden beyond the well's edge and focus on that, She thought. Let him see it there. Ensure that each of the teeny, tiny little steps toward the edge of the well and then up its side, that the man might make, occurred smoothly, and were pleasant to the man and rewarding.

This effort worked, for a time. It was, of all the ways The Woman tried, the most successful. It worked in fact, right up until the man came to the very edge of the well itself.

At this point, as he neared the well's edge, a strange thing happened.

At this point, the branches and roots that had been scratching him as they left his hands and feet, they became more noticeable.

As one left his right hand, it snagged at his wrist. It gouged at him and dug at his skin, bringing him to bleed, it drug along his wrist and would not be ignored. More drops of blood formed.

It was then, with his skin torn that he saw the well. He saw the whole of the wall of the well in its entirety.

And, despite the pleasantness of each step, which had been ensured by The Woman, he was, in this moment of vision, overcome with a terror that filled his eyes and caused them to open wide with the fear.

Perhaps he thought to scale it all in one bound, thought The Woman. For though She could see it was only three feet tall and held a garden and bounty beyond it, She knew that what *he* saw was fifty feet and more in height and was very dark indeed.

But I have ensured the pleasantness of every step, She thought to herself, surely he will trust Me further, to see that each step is small and continues to be joyful. And so She did not back away at his terror as perhaps She ought to have, for She was worthy of the trust he couldn't give.

As a result, with *this* attempt, She got kicked *and* bitten *and* lashed out at with both hands, which scratched her skin and tore it, making it bleed, making her heart hurt for him.

Let Go, She wanted to say, longed to say. Let Go of the roots, and the growing brambles.

For you can't get the benefit of trusting,

without trusting,

the benefit of letting go,

without letting go.

But, She knew now, from all that had occurred, that this he would never do.

*

It was then, at that very moment of dawning realization, as She stood with forearms bloodied, that She saw the veil.

For now was coming clear to her, the presence of a light veil upon him, that only now did he see. This thin film of veil blended with his skin and hair and eyes, it covered him at his eyes, his nose, and his mouth. Caught in the angle of light filtered through the dust around him, it was at first just a single glimmering, gilded edge. In a moment, it came to Her in its entirety, and She saw it.

Had it been this he'd been peaking around in those moments when it seemed he looked sideways out from his eyes? Could it be, *blind too*, this man in his well, flailing and kicking and holding too fast?

A peak out, sideways, offering him a briefest view, a snapshot, less even than that, outside, beyond the veil, She wondered? Did he look down at times, to see what lay beneath the veil and, doing that, did he catch a glimpse, a momentary sliver of the reality, the gardens, beyond the veil and beyond his well? Is this what he saw?

In again though, he would go. Tucking his head back behind the veil, he would return from the precipice of possibility that existed during his moments, his whisper-brief moments, of sightedness. It was a precipice of possibility which existed *only* during those brief moments.

What was it, She wondered, what could it *be,* that could possibly be *that* strong that it could pull him in again behind the veil in the face of such Potential, such ineffable beauty?

Then too, She saw more now, as if it was seeing his veil clearly that lifted the fog surrounding his well, to Her eyes.

For now She saw that on either side of the well … stood piles of dishes. She stared and stared. But indeed, high pile after high pile of cream-colored ceramic had stood behind the fog. Dirty piles seemed to be on one side, clean piles on the other. With feet in motion and while the God Seed and the man struggled in their well, *and* while the man held fast to the roots and branches of familiarity, he was *also,* She saw…

…toiling away at a task!

With his left hand he would reach up, and carefully balance a saucer or plate so as not to drop it to the bottom of his bottomless well (that was in reality not but three feet deep and was indeed not a well but his own body and soul.) He would wash the dish and then dry it as it passed first to his left foot, then to his right, then up to the right hand, to be placed finally, and ever so carefully, up on one of the high piles on the bank opposite.

The Woman was stunned.

Stupefied, She caught Her breath into Herself. What could this be about?

As amazing as this was to watch and as clever as he needed to be in order to complete such a cycle, a strange thing was happening, or not happening, to the piles as he worked.

Their levels, The Woman saw, were at no time altered.

The piles of dirty plates remained.

They remained exactly the same.

Their height was constant, not affected, in any way, by the toiling of the God Seed – their nature altogether unchanged. Lofty and tipping, threatening to topple, to crash and to break, the plates and the piles *did not stop* their tipping because of the man.

She saw that even during the light sleep that the manbody occasionally got, though he did not work on the plates directly, his body would however, remain engaged in these motions, endlessly cleaning and stacking dishes he never touched, engaged in the motion of it that would not let him be.

How, She wondered. *How did he do this?*

And, why? Whatever for? Why did he stay in motion like this, what caused it? What drove him? Was this, all of it, all simply so as to Not Lose Ground?

What possible energy could there be, with so much energy going to roots and treading and plates, left over for him, for other pursuits... for finding his garden? What energy for eventually finding the pathway behind his garden's last gate... and walking it?

But the cloud of fog surrounding him had lifted for Her and when She turned in a circle around Herself, She could no longer stop Herself from seeing what had been revealed there.

ALL of these others were there too. All of these beings like the manbody God Seed. And like this man, ALL of these others stood in wells of their own making. Each was treading water, and clinging to roots and branches, and each was engaged in a task.

All
     Of
        Them.

The tasks engaged in differed though. Some had dishes like the first man while others were pushing boulders endlessly up hills, the piles at top and bottom never changing.

She moved in closer, among the people, stepping around their wells. There were others, She saw, engaged in the fruitless nonsense of wiping themselves free of mud while in mud they were seated. Still others had papers, and they moved these papers from tray to tray, signing them, stamping them, placing them.

On and on it went, endless tasks endlessly performed.

Many actions, but the cycle and its end result in a task that never finished, remained constant for all.

As She walked, She reached out Her Hand. The Hand wiped clean the person where it touched, and it was in this way that She saw the tiny flickers of light inside those chests.

It was only when this happenstance of Hand touching chest had shown Her three of the lights flickering that She understood what they were.

She ran on ahead, touching each chest as she went. Each lit with a tremulous flicker of light as She did so.

The man had NOT been the only soul to have a God Seed which did not wither and die. All of them, every one, still had her or his God Seed inside of her or him! It was only that the light of theirs no longer shone outward like the welcoming, but weak, beacon of a lighthouse as his did. Despite the debris around it, his had remained lit, dimly, but lit nonetheless and it had been this that had been the difference that had stood him out from the rest.

For inside their wells and their tasks and their fear, all of them still had their God Seeds. Covered under by years of debris, their lights no longer flickered and the bodies around them were unaware of their presence, but indeed, they had not withered, they had not died.

A new joy formed in The Woman, mingling and melding with the joy already in Her: two sources, one life.

But, also, a new sadness formed too, for She was just beginning to see what her long journey would show her over and over, that it was not just this one man in his well, that they were *all* of them in their wells. He was alone in his well, but now She was more deeply recognizing that, in a completely different way, She too, was alone.

*

She had gotten in close to this man She had thought was a lone surviving God Seed, closer than others before her had. Because of that, She had seen.

He saw Her see and became jealous.

He had worked and worked at his task, as he was *supposed* to do, as he had been *told* to do, and it had not resulted in him seeing clearly. The Woman came along and simply saw clearly. He wanted that for himself. He wanted it very much. In fact he believed, he *deserved* it, *deserved* to see clearly.

And soon, his jealousy became anger and he had convinced himself he had never been jealous at all, but had only been *deserving* and so was justified, righteous, in his anger at her.

He lashed out at her with the root in his hand, and She saw that it was the one that had scratched the fear into him and had kept him from her and from his garden and had kept him too, from flying.

Her heart wept for him.

She turned once and her heart wept again, it wept this time for *all* the people and not just for him – for all their endless motion that held them down and kept them from the Truth.

And so, She walked on.

She knew She would have to now, for she had no plates, no branches, no boulders to push, no well, no mud, no tasks, no distraction from Truth. These cannot exist in the garden from whence the scent of the beginning comes.

And so, again, She walked on.

She walked,
        And She walked,
                And She walked.

*

And then, She sat.

She sat still.

She sat very still.

And She did this for a very long time.

And all the while that She sat, She sensed.

She did not think. She sensed and She sensed.

While the new moon came and went and the sun became sea, two sources, one life, She sensed.

And then,

all at once,

in Her stillness and sensing, She experienced again all the beauty and all the suffering that had ever been experienced.

Everything that had ever been experienced by anyone, all of it came to Her. This she both remembered and experienced for the first time.

Every act.

Every thought.

Every emotion.

Her lid protected her eye but this experience was completed before lash lowered upon lash. And though She had

had this experience many, many times, this time she understood something new from it.

When She understood, and only when She understood, She rose and made a decision.

She returned Her Spirit to the man then.

When She had with Her the consciousness of Her decision, Her spirit found again, the edge of that well which held the man and his God Seed.

In the flowers around her that She longed to but could not give him, Her spirit knelt.

And then, in total stillness, and without a sound, She lifted only a single Hand of her spirit.

And She held it out to the man.

She could not give him the garden, She could not give him peace. She could not show him even the ease of accessing Truth, and with Truth, of moving beyond the garden, for he was blinded by his veil and was held fast by his roots.

She could, however, give him this, and so She did.

The man took Her Hand and held it. In holding onto the Hand She'd lifted to him, he could *feel* much that he could not feel alone. Along with this heightened sense, though he could not receive peace, he did receive some little comfort.

Without a word, without even a sound, She left him then.

But, with him, She left a part of Herself, Her Hand, that he could see it, smell it, *feel* it.

She left it with him, that the God Seed within the man could know Her presence too.

As he held the Hand She had left him, a few of the flowers that surrounded her, and now surrounded the Hand, bent over themselves. They reached over from the edge. They touched up at the insides of his wrists then, lighting against the scratches there, and the scars.

He felt the beauty of that touch, the comfort. But too, immediately after that, he felt embarrassed. Embarrassed, that he had not been able to build his own garden. With the embarrassment, his jealousy of Her and of Her garden, became remembered.

Both emotions turned. They turned into the secondary experience that is anger and he barked and railed, lashed and swung out, wrapped inside the darkness of his fear. Later he would add his feet to the lashing and kick out at the Hand when he was jealous and embarrassed and because of those emotions, felt anger.

Of course, he could only kick out a little because he needed to keep them in motion and would drown of course, he thought to himself, were he to stop treading water.

But it was only the wind and Her Hand at which he lashed, because of course, She Herself had needed to go, for She knew now there were other souls to tend, other souls to know.

While She had to go, She left behind Her Hand, for what She had learned when She had gone away to sit and sense, was just this – that these beings, these people, none of them, *none* of them, knew about the pathway beyond the garden.

It was because of this that She understood the man needed to *see* the Hand, that he would need to see it there day after day after day, in rain and in sun, and despite his bad behavior which was designed to see if Her Hand would go away.

He needed, She understood now, to trust in that Hand and to trust in it solidly for though it was a quick and simple step out from where he was, She realized, *he* thought the Hand would have to hold him for a long, long climb. Had he awareness of the pathway beyond, he would know this to be a short and easy journey, but She now realized, he did not know.

He thought the Hand would need to hold him for a climb in which he would go up through the deep darkness of the long well and that he would be blind during this. And his legs, they were *tired*, so very tired and so he might need to rest. *He* thought he would need the Hand for all of that and so, for him, the Hand had to be very, very real.

But what She knew was this, that if ever he decided to believe in the Hand, or in himself, and grab hold of the edge or the wall of the well and begin to climb out, that the climb would not be as hard or take as long as wither assuring himself of success, or overcoming his fear had taken.

She knew that if ever he did that – believed in himself or in the Hand – then in one big step he would be up on the safe, level ground beside Her and that the well and the water which were in truth not even three feet deep and were only his own body and soul would be gone. She knew also that the muck covering the God Seed, that would all fall away and slough off too and it would be only the God Seed left, standing in its own Garden, seeing the pathway beyond it, and smelling of ancient richness beside Her.

*

In the moments when the man remembered to see the Hand, it was the God Seed that became Real and would in those moments, manifest its potential, which was something that he wanted but was also something too, that he feared a great deal.

In those moments when his eyes could see Her Hand and his brain registered its presence near him, well for those brief moments, he became greater than his fear. He became Real.

But as his constant motion distracted him and he lost sight of her Hand – which happened often – and in his distraction could also no longer feel its presence near him, well then in *those* moments the manbody with the God Seed inside it would fall backwards instead. It would be the well and the water in those moments that would become real then, its depth never-ending, the manbody falling, always falling.

She could not, she knew from trying, pull him up herself. But, she could leave Her Hand to hold his,

While he climbed out himself.

Through *that* ordeal, She could leave enough of Herself with him that he could feel Her there, standing beside him.

She thought of The Truth while Her Hand stayed beside him but Her life on earth continued elsewhere.

The Truth is, She thought, that we were, none of us, ever cast out of Eden.

Eden still is there, and we dwell there still. Right here, dwelling in Eden all of us, all along. It is, She sighed, only that we ceased to be able to see it, to perceive it all around us.

That is all that ever happened.

And so, She walked on.

Because She had to go.

But as She went, because he needed Her to stay, outward toward this being She had met, She held her Hand.

Though She went on, She was there beside him too – and *in*side him, for that, truly, is where the garden that is heaven lies.

He would see Her kneeling there, in the flowers, beside him, and always would. Her Hand held out.

Because,

      perhaps,

           one day,

     he would want to know the garden,

would want to experience the pathway behind the garden.

Perhaps,

      one day,

           he would seek to experience

The flight, the pain, and the beauty of all of humanity.

*

On and on She walked.

And as She walked, beings came to her: children, animals, seekers, empaths.

Many years before, when The Woman had been a small girl, it had happened to her, for her. The thing that had not happened to the man's God Seed – it had manifested.

When that had happened, She had fallen right through the garden and through the last gate, beyond which was a path.

Through that gate and onto that path, the same path that exists way out beyond the reach even of one's own memories, She fell, at the moment Her God Seed manifested.

She continued falling, and out beyond the reach of her own memories, She saw something else. This something else She saw had always existed but until now, She had been blind to its existence. But now, manifested, She saw it – the unbroken roots of the humanity organism.

She saw Herself fall past this winding tangle of unbroken roots upon unbroken roots. Roots that exist *between* beings, roots connecting beings, connecting Her and other beings, each to the other. Beyond *those* unbroken roots it was, that She fell right into the memories of another. She fell in fact, into the memories of *all* others.

For isn't it that which leads us most strongly to believe that we our discrete, our memories?

At that moment, She *experienced* the memories. All of them.

From inside this tangle of roots *between* beings, *of* beings, the appearance of separateness is removed and the vision of the one organism that is humanity is clear. On the pathway beyond the garden, all distinction, like all illusion and façade, is absent.

It is there, beyond that last gate, beyond the last path, that all that has ever happened to the humanity organism can be both remembered and experienced – all that ever was, is, and could be.

Since that time in Her early childhood, when her God Seed had Become Real, and even before that, beings had come to The Woman. Attracted by the garden and Her remembering, they came, yet wholly unaware of what it was that had attracted them there: children, animals, seekers, empaths, and more, so many, many more.

*

When the next day broke, The Woman watched each moment of its breaking. Her body did not try to coax movement from Her, nor did Her mind trick Her with pretensions of greater self-worth were She to be in motion.

It was because of these things about Her that the butter roses beside Her opened up their beauty for Her to see.

She breathed in the beauty that was given to Her as Her eyes breathed in of the rising sun.

As She sat, breathing in of beauty, of life, The Woman was aware of a Truth. And that Truth was that being alive meant that there was yet something for Her to learn – the kind of lesson that can only be *experienced*. While some things can be learned in many ways, other things can only be learned, She knew, through the experiences one was available to while in one of the iterations of one's body. In between journeys, *those* lessons could not be learned, because they could not be experienced.

The access to the garden and even to all that lay beyond it, had come to Her so easily, so clearly, indeed She had never been apart from it, disconnected from it. It was because of that clarity that She lived with confusion for why no others stepped out and accessed it as well, for why no others even saw.

She had learned recently that was the lesson She was here for, to experience an understanding of, a recognition of, and perhaps too, an empathy for.

*

She had come to recently understand this because of what She had seen beyond the God Seed's well.

For what The Woman had seen when She had walked away from his well each time, came to her now more clearly as She sat breathing in of the new day.

And what She had seen had been a shock to Her, a revelation.

For every time she stepped away from the well, a little clearer could She see what was around Her. About eight feet in every direction out from Her, was of course, a garden. But what She had not seen before She met the man, was that the eight feet were *moving with Her.* There was not garden everywhere, it was around Her only!

But now, when She walked, She could see indeed that the garden moved too. Because She now saw that, She looked toward the farthest edges of that beauty. Whenever She moved, and wherever She turned, there in the fog between the light of Her garden and the dark now beyond it, where the two met, She could now just, in that darkness, make out something there, something moving. Something in the dark beyond the light and the edge where light became dark, was moving, working.

Each time, She could see a little more, a little further into that gray. She could *understand*, with comprehension as newly dawning as the day, the degree of pain, that amount of fear, the struggle with which these God Seeds daily toiled. For there were people there, men and women, they were bent over, they were digging, digging in the mud. Some, in place of wells or mud around them, were danced about, puppet-like, suspended over flame. Others twirled helplessly in windstorms. Some were like electrons zinging, at the mercy of the chemicals inside them which sent them free-falling at high speed in new direction after new direction.

She had moved away from The People of The Wells and had now, in Her walking, come across the many other peoples of the many lands.

She strained to see, as She walked, just one who instead of digging, or zinging, or twirling helplessly, stood beside the mud instead, touching in a foot or a hand and, feeling the mud on their skin, remembered the way the mud feels. She strained to see just one other who, still enough to do so, lay in the grass admiring the underside of leaves.

Her garden moved with Her, and all these with God Seeds still hopeful inside of them, though they had their eyes open (flesh-colored veils still held fast in place of course) were, to Her dismay, sound asleep all.

And though the first set of still hopeful God Seeds struggled inside of wells, She had now walked long enough to have stumbled across other struggling peoples struggling in other ways.

It was then that She had walked away and sat. She sat for a long time. While She sat, She sensed. This was not something She worked at doing, but instead was a thing She could not stop from happening any more than She could stop this body in which She rested from breathing.

In the sensing, She went inside the man. In being connected to all things and aware of the connection, She could, with even light focus, experience what the God Seed man experienced in the well, what any of these beings in the hinterland beyond her Eden experienced.

She allowed Herself to feel this for a long time, to experience reality as it was perceived not by Her but by him.

When She had sat for a mark of time neither long nor short, She was aware of a sudden, that She understood, some little bit better.

First hand She experienced his fear, his terrible fear. She experienced his uncertainty, the uncertainty of living without her garden. To live without being able to sense the garden around you, or to feel the path beyond the last gate, or to know the record kept of all things for all time that lived along that garden's gated path, would be to live with pain such as She had never known. Despite all the bad that had happened to Her, She had always had the garden and Her sight, so though She knew pain well, *this* kind of pain was beyond all her previous knowing.

One would move not knowing, She thought. And in the next twinkling and of a sudden, She was warmed. It was the sudden onset of a deeper compassion – a compassion of vast immenseness, a new empathy born.

The compassion of this new understanding filled her completely, every cell, and didn't filter in a little at a time, warming her gradually, but immediately and all at once, filling Her with its warmth in a single instant.

It was then that She had stood.

And She had walked.

And She had walked into the dawn of this new day's beauty then.

*

The beauty of what each new day is, filled The Woman as the sun crested the horizon and She paused a moment as She did each day, sometimes many times in a day. For each day is nothing at all but infinite possibility, an infinite number of

Seeds of Possibility. So, to herself, in this pause, She repeated Her Thankfulness.

Thank you to the sunshine, good morning to the morning, thank you for this new day of possibilities, opportunities, and experiences for everyone.

On and on She walked.

And as She walked and beings came to her, She could too, feel the experiences of all those who'd come to her before and after.

In this way, She knew all, *felt* all, that was happening to the man, the first of the God Seeds She had met, as well as to all of the others She had met and not met.

Her pause completed, She continued her walking. But her thankfulness, that She carried with her as She carried all these other Seeds.

And as She walked, this feeling from the manbody came to Her.

She *felt* his experience. She felt it as it happened and She also felt his awareness that it had happened before many times. Every now and again it would happen as it was happening now – one of those near the God Seed, it always varied who, would gather together many words, construct from these a description, a possible explanation for this description, a *theory*. This one was telling, as the others had too, about an experience he had, a moment of Godness that had come to this being. He, or at times she, stood before the rest and began to share this litany of words in what they called talks, sometimes, lectures.

Wonderful and beautiful experiences, moments in time, these were conveyed to the others, including the man, in just this way.

The God Seed man was amazing at these times. He could remember every word of a talk, a lecture, or speech.

He couldn't *feel,* however, even one. She was feeling them through him, but he himself could not.

And he wanted that. More than anything he wanted to *feel* the *experience* of the words inside him, the experience the words conveyed.

He read too, the God Seed, to try to get that feeling. Book after book after book, he read of the beautiful moments of others, of their descriptions, and of the philosophies developed from those moments. Often he re-read and re-read again trying to pull from the words, the experience that they did not create in him.

But to him it would not come, his own personal moment of enlightenment, to be felt, experienced, remembered in the first person.

Occasionally, She knew, the man would run over to one of the others. Carrying his well with him, he would release his build-up of frustration in a torrent of scream. He would scream from within his well at all these others, at their descriptions of moments he could never have. He yelled out too at the Hand held out to him of course, but unlike these others, the Hand could not participate in the illusions of the man and so the screams fell short, eventually, fell silent before the Hand.

On other occasions, rarer still, he would reach his limits of another kind. His frustration with the limits he had put upon himself would join with the trust not so much in the Hand, but in what the Hand told him of Truth – that the climb would not be as hard as he thought it, as he envisioned it – and the joining of these two things would, for a quite rare moment, overcome his fear.

Then the man would gather his energy when this happened. He would prepare himself to let the plates fall, knowing he would have the noise of the crash to withstand. He would think about slowing his feet, about letting go of the roots and branches – first the left hand, then a foot, he would think.

But the slowing caused the careful functioning of the system to fall out of whack and in this way he came to understand that this move would need to be not slow, but all of a sudden, all at once, a fluid, flowing, united move. For this, he gathered himself up.

It was then that the weirdness began.

A dozen of those closest to him, those who he had selected and *allowed* to be near him, specifically for their willingness to participate in his illusions and to keep him from the danger of these very moments, would run over then, from the wells around his. Just as he was up against his edge, ready to leap and let the plates crash, to let the roots and branches drop and in one swift jerky motion vault himself out from the well and onto the solid land and garden beside it, these nearest others, they would make their move just then.

They would run over, as he would have made the vault,

to keep him from it and pull him back.

The man had chosen these beings to be around him specifically *because* he knew they would pull him back. He knew they would remind him that the well was alright, that it was not limiting, that he was, at least, alive in the well and too that he couldn't know what was waiting for him out there beyond it. So, to him, because of this, their actions were of course, no surprise at all.

To the Woman, this first time seeing it, and not knowing the authority even from which those others felt justified in interjecting their thoughts, their feelings, or opinions on his actions, their behaviors were, at first, quite a great surprise indeed.

Stay, they told him, pulling him back from the vaulting with their own hands which were roots and brambles and branches of hands.

Oh, that was close, they said then. *We are here to support you, to keep you from pain.*

The Woman, in seeing the great toil and pain and sadness of the man in the well, was confused at first. But soon She saw that it was indeed their own fear of their own pain that caused the words and the actions of those near the man. For, if the man succeeded, they would be forced then, each of them, to face their own fears and their own growth.

Understanding this, compassion was greater still.

In sitting, She was able to send out from herself, Her comfort to the man. So this She did.

Do not worry, She told the man *I will still be here, when you are ready. Whenever you are ready to wave aside these wizened others and not be held back, I will be here for you still.*

Quietly, She told the same to all the others, those who were unaware that their pedestal of compassion was no more than crutches.

When She had begun walking, She had walked south and so had come upon the God Seed and his well and that well had been beside a vast and unending body of water that sang directly into her of limitlessness, boundlessness.

It spoke too, of the inseparable nature of the drops of water that formed this sea.

Then She had turned, walking east from there.

And, She walked on now.

Although, still, a part of Her stayed behind, as it always would – Her Hand, held out, would stay always beside him. Though She went on, She was there beside him too. He would see Her kneeling there, in the flowers, beside him, and always would. Her Hand held out.

Because,

      perhaps,

           one day,

he would want to know the garden,

would want to experience the pathway behind the garden.

Perhaps,

      one day,

           he would seek to experience

The flight, the pain, and the beauty of all of humanity.

*

On and on She walked.

And as She walked, beings came to her: children, animals, seekers, empaths.

After She had crossed a tremendous set of magnificent mountains – beautiful in their crags, differently so in their meadows – there was one who came to Her who asked of her a question. It was a question She had, when She'd been in a much younger body, contemplated once or twice, though the question then had taken other forms and come to her in different words, for the answer was so obvious.

And now, with this question, She was given a new form of understanding. She was given a chance now, to understand better, the tasks She had witnessed – those endless tasks at which these beings were engaged. All the beings – busy at the folding, the pushing, the lifting, cleaning, stacking, writing, busy at the tasks that kept them from themselves.

What do you want?

And with that, it was there for her – the explanation.

They kept away from themselves because they didn't know – They didn't know what to want.

He wore a veil. He toiled. Around him there was no desert and no well of water. Around this God Seed there was a storm of winds, a tremendous crash and swirl of winds. At times, the noise of the storm would deafen him. At other times, it was the freezing temperatures of the winds themselves which would burn him.

This one, he walked along beside Her as she moved. She looked at him a long, long time when he asked Her that. She looked at him as they walked, sensing him with her gaze and with the rest of her.

What She sensed very clearly was that he wouldn't understand.

She could have told him to

Start with the non-linearity of time
and then, stop thinking.

That would have been enough for him to have felt good about, to have moved on with.

But She also sensed that, unlike most, this one, while not understanding, would not be afraid either.

His lack of understanding would not upset him.

This was important. She did not want to bring pain.

It was there though, present in him.

And so She told him.

She told him as clearly, as briefly, as artfully as She could, the answer to the question he himself had asked Her.

First, She cautioned him, *sentences,* She said, *that begin with* I want *are dangerous sentences indeed. Rephrase your question when asking it of yourself.*

Then, She began.

She began with:

> Start with the non-linearity of time
> and then, stop thinking.

She continued with:

> Because after that,
> the rest must be sensed.

Then, She said to him all the rest, though She knew he would not understand.

There is a garden one carries with one, She said. *In this garden is a gate. It is not a secret gate. It is clearly marked.*

For there are no secret Truths.

People quest to find the garden, but you can't quest for it, it is right there. Everyone has one – both a garden and a gate. To

*journey and seek would be to move away from it. All one has
to do, all one* can *do is open one's eyes.*

*People try to seek out teachers, try to learn how to get to
the garden by following a teacher to a destination.*

But it cannot be learned.

*One cannot follow or lead, one can only help in the way of
reminding others of what they already know – and anyone can
do that, one does not need a teacher in order to be reminded.*

Here She paused. The two sat together beside a gentle
creek. From this She filled her drinking vessel and drank of
the clear water. Then, since still he was quiet and still he was
listening, and still he remained unafraid, She continued.

Beyond this gate, She said, *is the pathway to human
oneness, the pathway to the one humanity organism of which
we are a part.*

*All of human experience is available to each of us beyond
this gate.*

Everything that has ever happened, and has ever been felt.

*Along the path beyond this gate, one can fly without
moving.*

*Far from the garden, one can travel, and into any
experience or location or knowledge that has ever been held
in any mind.*

I fly out of the garden, from the path beyond the gate.
When I fly, I experience what has been recorded.

I come back with renewed wisdom for having experienced
someone else's pain one time, beauty through another's eyes
another time, the value judgment of one inducing the suffering
of another on a visit elsewhere.

All people have access to this pathway and the record it
bears and since they do, I would like it if more people
remembered to access the gate, and then the pathway. That is
what I would like.

I can open that gate, I can slide into the tangle of unbroken
roots that is the humanity organism, and though many souls,
many animals, many flowers, are on that path and surround
me with joy,

I am as alone on that path as I am in the garden.

For I have yet to find another soul resting inside a human
vessel, that can access the pathway. So though I am not lonely
in the way that others are lonely, there is instead a big L sort
of Loneliness.

I would like to live, here on earth, among other souls like
mine, souls who, like me,

Can live in Eden without destroying it.

For those who can fly free from the path among both beauty and pain, return again, and do both without losing themselves.

There is another, one only perhaps, but at least one, who dwells in human form, who can join me on that path and in that flight. I had thought, when young, that there were many.

I had thought it was everyone.

But, though everyone is born with this capacity, most remain incapable of accessing it.

And so I walk, I walk that I might one day, come across this one other soul, dwelling also in human form.

The two of us together, despite the distance between us, would fly then, and dance together, our minds connected in the same joy, experiencing the same remembered record of past, future and always – Two Minds Flying, Two Minds Dancing.

Here, She paused, She thought about his words, his language. *That is to say, in your language, to be loved not for body nor chemistry, nor for any electron-like zinging. To be loved beyond reach of culture or parenting, society or teaching or happenstance. Two Minds, Together.*

Soaring.

And let the soaring be higher, longer, stronger and freer than is either of the two minds capable of, on its own.

Here, She paused again. She sipped some water, then he did the same. She was not harming him with dissonance, so She felt safe in continuing and sipped again before speaking.

I will be free from the cycle of re-birth whenever I shall pass from this body. Before that, there is this opportunity that I describe. With this, we two joined can shift from observance to effect. We can create change – small at first for certain but perhaps with luck, with practice, larger in time. Then this thing created can go out into the world, to make that small ripple that slightly alters the path of the humanity organism, making wider ripples – circular waves in size ever growing – in that path outward from it as it goes.

Romantic love is but a microcosm of this – instinctive re-creation of something larger. For it is not the big L Loneliness which causes the want, it is

The desire to remember again,

that which I was sent to remind.

That is what I would like to see. One day, perhaps, if I dwell in this body long enough, it would be nice. But that is very different from I want, *which is a dangerous way to start a thought.*

And so She had shared with him.

She shared with him what it was he had asked for her to share.

And he did not understand.

The Woman had not expected him to.

She stopped speaking and ate of the food before her for She had answered his question as clearly, as briefly, and as accurately as the limits of words acting on concepts that cannot be described will allow.

He could not understand.

It was not because of the words that he did not, but because he could not perceive any of the concept's parts described by the words.

This She had expected. It did not alarm or trouble her. One cannot grasp the immensity of what is beyond a door apparently, if one has not sensed the presence even of the door.

Some things, The Woman knew, were

Just too big to be seen,

Just as some things were too small. Though it was right in front of him and handed to him gently on a nicely summed up metaphorical platter, he could not yet see it. For he was looking with his eyes. And his mind. But,

> For one's eyes to open to Truth,
>
> one must look with Compassion.

So he walked without grasping.

But, in this one, She had hope.

Feel it, She whispered.

And though he did not hear, some part of him did, She knew.

The God Seed walking beside her walked a long while without speaking. Then he said, *That is more words than you have spoken in the week I've walked along with you, so I will think on them with the respect that warrants.*

She had known he would. With a chuckle She added only to herself, *and more words too than you will hear for another week.*

The God Seed's chuckle was added to her own and together it became laughter.

But tell me, asked this God Seed, *if you did not hope for me to understand, then why did you share?*

Because, said The Woman, *I hoped for hope.*

And so She walked on.

*

On and on She walked.

And as She walked, beings came to her: children, animals, seekers, empaths.

As She walked, She sensed her body - felt Her breath coming in, going out. Felt the air moving in Her lungs, in Her blood, listened to Her heart beating, felt the rumblings of hunger in Her stomach, felt her skin, toes, hair. She reveled in each. At the same time, She listened around Herself as well. High up, She heard the melodic warbling of the Meadowlark followed by another. Was the beauty of their communication – one call requesting information, asking, and a second beautiful song giving it, replying – matched by the beauty of the messages; the information of every day, exchanged in poetry and accompaniment?

Redwing blackbirds, magpies, raptors, these were there too. Down lower, below them here, sparrows, bluebirds, finches and nuthatches added to frogs and crickets and the shrieks and laughter of children playing. She felt the cawing of the magpies, their long iridescent blue tails of royalty behind them, as they squabbled over peanuts tossed from a gray-haired bench sitter smiling at them. The water of the creek roaring at its middle yet lapping at the shoreline, the crunch of bicycle tires on gravel, another part of the creek falling down in uniformity to a lower river, the splash of a fish jumping, these things She heard, and She felt, as She walked on.

But, as She went, though She felt and listened both inside and outside Herself, outward too, toward this new God Seed She had met and just parted from, She held Her Hand.

For She had not held out Her Hand to the man in the well only, She had held out all Her Hands. She held them out to all the people of all the world, to all people everywhere She held out all Her Hands, because of all of their fear.

So, though She went on, She was there beside this new God Seed too. He would see Her kneeling there, in the flowers, beside him, and always would. Her Hand held out.

Because,

      perhaps,

           one day,

he would want to know the garden,

would want to experience the pathway behind the garden.

Perhaps,

      one day,

           he would seek to experience

The flight, the pain, and the beauty of all of humanity.

*

On and on She walked.

And as She walked, beings came to her: children, animals, seekers, empaths.

This night it was the woman, Fatima, who was called and who stopped beside Her.

When Her stomach asked Her to, She stopped and ate a small dish of rice. Before She pulled this from the small pack at Her back, She first found a source of water to sit by. On this night it was a large creek, further up on the same swollen creek beside which She'd eaten last evening's meal. Other times the water beside which She sat was a pond, or a small lake.

Though a tree nearby was always an added blessing for Her meal, She sought out places for this part of the day that were not blocked in by the presence of many trees as in a forest, places where the whole of the western sky could be observed without obstacle if possible.

She sat then, spot located, feet folded under, and ate of Her rice. When the grains were consumed, She rinsed the bowl and fork in the creek as She'd done the night before, and returning them both to the pack, She sat, quiet before the show about to start for Her in the western sky.

She did not think during this time. Nor did The Woman use this time to process the day. She simply watched and simply listened. It was not just the show made by the sun that She watched, but also the children nearby, playing in water as they always have and always will. She felt the beat of Her heart and again the feel of Her lungs filling.

And though it was with an attention that included things that another might be able to tick off a list – saw the reds, caught all the many shades of pink that mingled and built, noted the amazing cloud formations off to the left, appreciated the way the colors bounced off of the cloud and the way that changed throughout the show – the attention itself was of a different material, a far finer yet more nebulous, even ineffable, material than that which would have created a list. It was of a material that let her not only fully, truly *see* the show, and not only then to keep it with her always, but also of a kind that allowed her to build her own materials and to build her own show; a microcosm, a smaller cosmos, an inner version of the outer beauty, to carry *that* with her too and build a garden in it.

It was the same material that allowed her to know that outside the gate, in that garden, lay the path that would take one past the unbroken roots of humanity that connected us each to the other. It was the same material that allowed Her to know that if one could just see past that gate, could just recognize the roots of connection, that it would be there on the path that lay all of human experience – beauty and suffering – readily available and easily accessed.

It was the same material out of which was built the love of The Woman that was both for each being and at the same time, for the humanity organism.

After the show had faded and passed, it was often the case that She would sit longer, now sensing inwardly in the darkening space around Her. In years past, She sensed what She could of the outward world, of outward reality. Now though, it was of these other beings who shared the lightened space, the darkened space, and the space of all shadows between, that She sensed.

Where were the assumptions that had turned them in the wrong directions? These assumptions were there, somewhere, hidden in the interpretations that created false emotions, hidden in the thought-strings that moved them, moved some to fear and moved fear to anger. She couldn't help unless She could undo the assumptions. But, She couldn't do *that* unless She could find them, drawing them first out into the light, where their undermining limitations would be made as clear as their erroneous application. Into the light where the too general application of them, the sloppy pigeon-holing which lacked judiciousness and had led to grievous error, could be readily recognized.

It was during this hour of the evening when day became night; two sources, one life, that though She sat often in shadow, She was sought out by many – squirrels, finches, once an owl, many pets, toddling children, and of course many, many people.

On this summer evening, beside the raging energy of the white-capped creek, She felt the approach of one who held within her a material of a quality the slightest bit finer than that of the well dwellers and the foot burners. This one, though not having found yet the gate or the garden path beyond it, had indeed managed nonetheless, to have built around herself, a fine garden. This meant that the veil had fallen away from her and that she could see.

The Woman opened Her eyes.

Hello, She said.

Hello, said the other woman quietly, without surprise.

With the others, The Woman had been able only to listen and to reply, but not to be seen. She knew that while this new other was not yet The One Other with whom she could experience Two Minds Dancing, with this one She would be able at least, to be seen. And this was enough, so much more than enough.

I am Fatima, the girl told The Woman. *My man has gone in search. He will be back, in this life or the next, it makes no difference.*

Yes, many, they feel they must search it seems, The Woman answered.

He will find his grail where he left it, said the girl.

Just as in all the search stories, agreed The Woman.

The treasure, and here the younger woman made little gestures, marks in the air with her fingers, *is always right there, with them all along. Get back home and man or woman, they find what felt so distant.*

False grails, if only people could remember this, whispered The Woman. To this, Fatima nodded.

Only a fool leaves a treasure to seek
a smaller treasure..

The two nodded in shared sadness at the inability of people, to remember.

Still, Fatima added as they walked,

there are so many fools.

The Woman knew that when they parted, and this woman traveled with Her in Her heart only, that Fatima's would be an existence that would warm Her at the thought of it out there in the world, just being.

The two walked along in peaceful silence together for a long while then.

It was my brother, the girl said, speaking as though to continue a thought they'd both had, though it had been hours since words had passed between them. *He walked along with you, a short time. You told him of the gate beyond the garden. He said I would find you here, where I found you.*

Ah, him. The Woman smiled. *He was without fear that one, without anger at the things he does not understand.*

It's true.

This is rare in your beings, I think.

Yes.

And you are like him in this.

Yes.

Though too, you, I think, understand a bit more even than your brother.

She walked along with this one. They walked along together, by the creek, for two days. After which, they parted company.

I will tell my father, the Colonel, of our visit, Fatima called out to her as they parted.

Yes, The Woman said.

And so She walked on.

But as She walked on, outward toward this being She had met, She held Her Hand. She did this

Because,

     perhaps,

          one day,

she would want to know the garden,

would want to experience the pathway behind the garden.

Perhaps,

one day,

she would seek to experience

The flight, the pain, and the beauty of all of humanity.

*

On and on She walked.

And as She walked, beings came to her: children, animals, seekers, empaths.

As She walked too, The Woman observed inwardly to see what, if anything, the experiences of those two days had changed in her. Was something made more possible, less possible?

But as She sensed and walked, it was the soul of the manbody, the God Seed in his well, who came to her this night. She heard him, *felt* him. He was engaged in an uncertainty. It was the uncertainty that is the process of readying himself to put something into words. This something he was struggling to put into words, was readying himself to put into words, was an intimacy, a quiet reflection, which he had not shared before, not given voice to before, perhaps not even realized before today.

Instantly, She was there with him, returned, beside him, because of his readiness, though She was with her body on Her walk at the same time.

I want, he began unsteadily, hesitantly.

What I want, he tried again, *is to know, to know the whole picture, how it all fits together, the true nature of all reality and what it all* means.

There are many who are like you in this, She said, comforting the man.

Yes, the manbody said, *but I, I would like to know this all, for fear of making a wrong step, before I take that first step.*

I see, said The Woman who knew this about him but who was happy for *him* that *he* had found the error in his efforts, the application of fear where better his massive discipline would have been applied.

So, now you will know to move, to move not in place and use your discipline to tread water, but to now, take a step. Do that, take that step you need to take, and use your discipline to quell your fear.

The God Seed prepared himself, he coiled internally and externally, mentally he prepared himself for the tightening of the brambles at his wrists, the roots at his ankles. He prepared himself for the rising and crashing of the water. Most of all, he prepared himself for those he had selected to be around him, to withstand the onslaught of their good intentions.

She held his hand, that was caught fast at the wrist and She whispered to him reassuringly. The water rose, the noise with it, till it became deafening. The roots pulled and the people nearby, getting wind of what was planned, rushed close.

The people nearest, just on cue, began to whisper, began to yell, began to pull at the man. His courage and his trust in himself and in Her, shrank then just a bit, but when he needed those things most. Seeing this, The Woman spoke.

It is true that not all who wander are lost. But it is equally true that not all who are lost, wander. Stand and find yourself.

And with that, the coiled man released the coil and burst forth. For a moment, the briefest of moments, he was out of the well and on his knees in a field of flowers and green grass, cooled by a lovely breeze. He began slipping back into the well immediately, but while he slipped backwards, he looked around himself. For the first time in his life, he smiled a true smile.

He was back inside the well, his legs moving wildly, his hands reaching for familiar holds, before the smile was complete. However, She saw that he was now much closer to the well's surface than he'd been before his effort. His head and eyes just poked out above the surface edge of it now. All looked the same and yet, all was changed now.

And it would be that which would make all the difference in his life She knew, for it is not those who are ten steps distant that the other beings would look to for leadership, but those who are only one step distant, one step closer to the surface of the well.

And so She walked on.

But as She walked, outward to the man She held Her Hand. As She walked, onto the wind She whispered to the man so that one day he might feel the Truth of Her words. She whispered:

It Will All Be Alright.

These things She did because She knew that he *did* want to know the garden, he *did* want to know the pathway beyond, he *did* want to know the record that is the record of all the beauty and all the pain of all that is and ever has been the humanity organism.

*

On and on She walked.

And as She walked, beings came to her: children, animals, seekers, empaths.

The being who came to Her this night was Of The Mud. That is, he was one of those engaged in the task of wiping himself free of mud, the very mud in which he sat, slept, ate - lived.

This being came to Her as She sat still by the water.

She sensed clearly, immediately, that this Mudder was different, that inside *this* Mudder was recognition of something, was pain because of this recognition. Inside this Mudder was recognition that the world, the Truth, around him was somehow, in some way, *different* than that which he had been told. He perceived things differently than that way in which he had been told to perceive the world, and in that crack, in which he saw a glimpse of Truth beyond what he'd been told, was his pain – the pain of his dissonance – and it was that which started the process for him, of weaving a stronger self of a stronger material. He was no longer of these others. He was beginning to wipe the mud off of himself in a more permanent way.

Yet, leaning around him, She could see that, behind him, *something,* something was happening. This something struck her as more inexplicable even than what went on around the other God Seeds.

Here, She saw behind this one, clearly, that the people Of The Windstorms were, well it looked as though they were *terrorizing* the people Of The Mudswamps. Running at each other, shrieking, yelling, ranting, waving arms and legs and weapons!

What was this? wondered The Woman.

Beyond *that,* She saw, leaning around the Mudder to his other side, that it *also* appeared, in fact quite plainly, as if the people Of The Mudswamps were terrorizing the people Of The Windstorms right back. Indeed, they were!

The Woman returned then, to her seated position behind the Mudder who had come to Her.

Help Us, begged the Mudder before Her.

Why do they do this! She asked him. *Why do they do this each to the other?* The Woman asked again. *Why is it they do not struggle* together?

But, The Mudder had no words for her and so they sat and both of them together, they watched, they listened.

As The Woman listened, She became aware of slight differences, nuances in the words, the terms, that the Mudders were using and that the Stormers were using.

The concepts each was expressing – these were the same. But the terms each group used to express the same concepts – these differed.

And what it was that struck The Woman most, about the differences, was this.

The differences in the terms had been developed, not to clarify communication,

But to exclude.

The terms of one group did not clarify Truth or represent Truth better or more fully, they were designed, and then reinforced and strengthened simply to exclude some people, include others,

And to identify each!

The terms were used, each by each group, to separate, to identify, to feel a part of something by first ensuring that something, someone, *some entire group of someones* just like oneself, was excluded. For these beings thought that,

To feel *included,* one must first identify those to be *excluded.*

The terms for concepts, even the norms of behaviors, had developed not to clarify, not to connect, but to separate and identify! Her mind was boggled by this state of affairs almost beyond endurance. *What could be gained by such small, such ridiculous, indeed such petty feelings of inclusiveness?*

And who was here to count the cost, the staggering, mind numbing cost? Indulgence – such cost, so little gain.

And then, as they sat watching and with no warning at all, She was attacked! Both She and the Mudder who was clearly also not of them any more than She, were attacked as they sat together observing, harming no one.

Though the two were under the protection of Her mind, a mind which had gone beyond the pathway and returned, and could therefore suffer no blows upon them, A Mudder and a Stormer, together, both attacked the seated two. Each attempted to beat with fists, strike with weapons, and rage into the seated faces the anger they had rationalized themselves to be deserving of.

Each had seen a being that was not of their grouping and determined that to mean She must be of the other group – for that was the purpose of their words, their markings, their norms and mores. Each group so imbued of its own lens – a lens each reinforced by its own terms – that the possibility that an Other could come along who did not fit into its pre-made categories, was lost.

All other alternative possibilities
were Inconceivable, even... Unperceivable

And this, She saw as She sat there with unsuccessful blows
directed at her, was the worst of it, the very worst. That lost
along with the rest of the things, was even the very *possibility*
of one day, perceiving correctly.

Gone the possibility to sense the inaccuracy that existed, to
sense not *what* the alternative lenses showed, *but even* that
alternative lenses existed.

She spoke to them. She reached out to them. She reached
first with Her mind, then with Her Heart which wept for them.

The lenses were too thick, too strong, too reinforced. The
fear to set the lenses down simply too solid – so solid it
created a wall. It was a wall too high, and was one through
which these beings could no longer hear, or see, or feel. They
could not even perceive Her any longer.

She and the Mudder, an empath and of stronger material,
the two moved away from these then.

The two walked together for another day and then they
parted as well.

And so She walked on.

But as She went, outward toward these, She held Her
Hand. Though She went on, She was there beside them too.
Each would see Her kneeling there, in the flowers, beside him,
and always would. Her Hand held out.

She did this
      Because
           one day,
                they might seek to experience

The flight, the pain, and the beauty of all of humanity,

    To experience the beauty that is the organism
              that is humanity.

*

On and on She walked.

And as She walked, beings came to her: children, animals, seekers, empaths.

And as She walked, and the garden moved with her, She smiled the smile of inner peace and not of external happiness. She said her morning Thankfulness to the new day.

Thank you to the sunshine, good morning to the morning, thank you for this new day of possibilities, opportunities, and experiences for everyone.

She walked past many souls as She went. All of these souls, be they inside vessel bodies of the female label or the male label, were heavy in veil – Lens covering eyes directly, or cloth needing to be looked through, both kinds of veil. In addition, some were digging at the dirt beneath them. Deep inside their private wells clinging fast to familiar roots and branches were many others, spread flat in desert sands still others. Some wept, others cheered, still others, sweat-stained and grime-covered, choked on the dust floating up from their toil. A few even, had small levers they had rigged, which gave off smoke and it was, for these, thinking themselves progressed, on this smoke that they choked.

Now as She walked though, She noticed small piles that before She had not noticed. Little piles, in and around the deserts and wells and muds in which stood the men and women She observed at the outskirts of Her garden.

The piles, they were of GIFTS.

Stacked high in piles and with beautiful shapes and sizes, textures and colors, were these gifts.

The people though, they

Walked *around* the piles, the gifts.

The people, struggling, paid no attention to the gifts and even turned the other way, toward some other task, their task of eternity perhaps, any task, *almost as if to avoid having to look at the beauty of the gifts.* To The Woman, the beings gave the sense that the tasks must have seemed of more value than the gifts from which they turned.

Again, The Woman was baffled by the beings of this land. Again, The Woman struggled, both to understand and to find a way to show or tell these beings that She met.

She observed these piles, these gifts ignored, as She walked.

And then, walking a bit further, *Ha ha ha*, laughed The Woman and She bent over doubled at the waist.

She laughed a laugh that was a sound as hearty and yet as peaceful as that of the earth breathing, as of all among it exhaling in unison. But it was the sound of sadness too.

For there, in the gifts and the piles, being ignored by those hard at labor and heavy in veil and lens, who walked around them toward lesser prizes, were indeed, yes –

The Keys to the Kingdom,

The Pathways to the Pathway,

The Catalysts to the Alchemy

The key, the *access*, which led to the pathway whereupon one's veil and lens and root and branch would fall away, sat untouched, covered in dust and debris, among the piles and amid the unopened packages.

The access to the pathway beyond the garden was hidden, as it always is and always would be, in plain view. And there sat the very keys to that access, as the beings picked their way around them.

She laughed and it was the sound of beauty, of loam becoming trees.

But it was also the sound of sadness, the sound of one man crying.

Because laughter and sadness are but two skins – two sources, one life.

The gifts, *opening them,* even seeing them, perceiving their presence, would lead one to the garden, and then, to the Pathway beyond – the path to the path.

She laughed while the tears
slid down Her cheeks.

And She walked on.

*

On and on She walked.

And as She walked, beings came to her: children, animals, seekers, empaths.

As She walked this day, She came upon two beings.

The two men were fighting, engaged in heated exchange.

It was their assumptions which divided them – the same assumptions so opaque to The Woman.

The son of one, the daughter of the other, they wished to marry; the first a Mudder, the second fumbling above fire.

As the Woman listened further, She came to understand from their words, that which perhaps the two men did not.

She understood from that implied in this union of young people, there was a suggestion, a suggestion neither wished to be confronted with, and that to these two men was quite painful indeed.

It is a suggestion of value,

Said The Woman to the fighting men who sought her out.

It is a suggestion of value where none had been seen, a suggestion of worth, quality, deservedness, acceptance, even of beauty, seen, each in the other, which unseats you both.

This suggestion insulted the fire dancer.

This suggestion insulted the mudder.

Inside of the insult was fear – for they had each behaved badly toward the other group time and again, and if in fact, the other groups each were worthy, what then of their bad behavior? What then of the pain each had inflicted upon the other?

The mudder, and all his allies, donned in fact, suits of special clothing symbolic of the differences separating the groups. In this way, he meant to let it be known he would not forget, and in remembering, would allow the mistakes and pains of the past to create more mistakes, more pains, in the present.

With this suit, he stated boldly, that he would in fact, be also happy to *force* these present mistakes into being, to create them himself, were additional mistakes with further damage not forthcoming in the present on their own.

Now, the mudder did not see that the suggestion had also insulted the fire dancer who for his part, and wearing his only special, symbolic clothing making the same statement, did not notice that the mudder had also become enflamed by what the young love implied.

For they lacked humility.
And so, together, they built

The Narrative of Aggression.

Each needing the other for the build-up – action,
judgement, arrogance, reaction.

The Woman spoke then.
To each, She said these things, telling what She saw.

And then She walked on.

Many months it would take, for comprehension to
transform Her words into understanding, many more years
after that, for understanding to become compassion.

Until that transformation occurred,
She could do no more.
After it, no more would be needed.

For either, Recognition would need to come first. And that
had already been brought to them, by their children – children
who had become clear-sighted to the Truth of worth and value.

And so She walked on.

But as She went, outward toward these beings she had met, She held Her Hand. Though She went on, She was there beside them too. Each would see Her kneeling there, in the flowers, beside him, and always would. Her Hand held out.

Because,

       perhaps,

           one day,

one would want to know the garden,

        one might want to experience the pathway

        beyond the garden.

Perhaps, one day,

        one would seek to experience:

The flight, the pain, and the beauty of all of humanity.

*

On and on She walked.

And as She walked, beings came to her: children, animals, seekers, empaths.

She had walked into the Gulf of Mexico and there, She sat. Into the shimmering sunrise of a new day She gazed.

It was there that the creature called dolphin found her.

And She knew the creature and the creature knew Her.

There was no pretense in the creature, no pretense that it did not sense this recognition, no pretense that the communication that occurred between them did not occur and so,

Because the pretense of impossibility was absent,
the possible transpired with ease.

Mind to mind, without words, without hesitation, their communication transpired.

Instantaneously.

Completely.

The instantaneousness of it did not upend the creature called dolphin, did not unsettle its understanding of time, creating from that fear the secondary emotion – anger.

Though it took but a moment, She stayed by this being called dolphin until sunset. Together they shared the experience, the joy, the beauty and fullness that is Two Minds Dancing.

When the last of the rays of the last of the colors had blended into the sea and they were in darkness fully, they parted.

The dolphin returned to its family and deeper waters, and The Woman rested and then walked on.

But when She walked on, She carried this being with her as She had carried with Her all the other beings She had met and not met.

The communication did not end because of the distance that grew with each step of hers, with each splash and kick from the dolphin, but remained steady, easy, real.

And so She walked on.

And as She walked, outward toward this being She had met, She held Her Hand. Though She went on, She was there beside him too. He would see Her kneeling there, in the flowers, beside him, and always would. Her Hand held out, even though this one already knew about the garden.

*

On and on She walked.

And as She walked, beings came to her: children, animals, seekers, empaths.

This day as She walked, it was a man-body who approached and walked with Her. He brought his well with him, and he brought his fire also. But he brought along mud and wind and papers upon papers needing stamping too. The papers were not in stacks.

This one has been badly hurt, She thought. She felt of his heart as well, and knew it to be of a special warmth, a deeper openness. For this, She hoped She would be able to remind him of something that would be of help to him, of use in his growth or in its permanence.

She was interested to better understand the dissonance of this beautiful but peace-less being. She gestured to the being and the being sat. The process of unlearning Truth, of forgetting, that begins in childhood, leaves dissonance behind it. Through Her years of walking, She realized that it was greatest in those who were the best of these beings. The dissonance of this one was great indeed.

He sat somewhat near Her and they stayed like that, in meditation together, and after a time She came to the greater understanding She had sought.

Ah, She said then, *it is a form of repression, even oppression, that you feel.*

Yes, said this being, *That is it, that is it exactly.*

As always happened when Her movement stopped or shifted, crowds began to gather. Around them now as they sat, people came, one at a time, and they lingered. Many sat with them.

If I understand correctly, you think that there is a type of "wildness" to your masculinity that at times is repressed, stifled, by civilization, by domestication.

Indeed! Exactly! Help me, please, would you?

There are, my child, three sources of illusion to this feeling that for you is so strong it blocks all else coming from you.

Three, Rinpoche? Is there hope for me then?

You may hope for hope, always.

Please, then, please, teach me the sources of my pain, that I may hope to begin.

I cannot teach, but I like you, can help by reminding and I will you remind you of these things.

The DISSONANCE you feel is your recognition
of the lenses which veil your eyes.

There is room in your life and in your spirit, for
wildness and orderliness both.

SEEK BALANCE in your life.

And, most important of all, remember that this has

nothing at all to do with your MASCULINITY.

Do not be fooled, young man, for there is a place for you that
is wild and free and always has been and that place is beside
another mind, raising your family together and always has
been.

But I have no family save my wife, Said the manbody.

And your place is beside your wife – your wild *place. But,*
your family *is all around you, it is whomever touches your life*
that you may touch back, heart to heart, reaching out in
kindness and compassion.

I see, said the being, *but this though, is of a wildness*
woman cannot possibly understand.

Wildness, said The Woman, *is a* HUMAN *experience – not a* MALE *experience. All humans are capable of understanding all that is within human experience, do not limit yourself so.*

If there are no secret Truths, then there are also no secret understandings knowable by only one gender, or by any subgroup.

Man, woman, male and female, The Woman said, *these are not opposites, my child, they are not even different. They are one. Please, the illusions, they fool you, separate you. They keep separating until you feel alone and in your alone-ness you seek a group – a group of "sameness."*

The Winders, the Stormers, The FireDwellers and WellDwellers, these too, they feel this same way, this way you feel, but none of theirs is true either, no more true than your thought here.

The TRUTH *is this,*

You were never alone

and never separate.

The truth is this as well, that yin and yang do not represent strength and weakness, they

Honor different kinds of strength.

Day and night do not represent light and dark, they

Honor different kinds of light.

It is this same with the bodies, the vessels on this earth, which house your souls, our souls.

They aren't opposites, they never were, male and female are only terms. The bodies, they're not even separated, we are all one – one humanity organism. How then could two within that organism, be opposites?

Within the spectrum that you label gender, there are enormous numbers and versions of strengths and light.

Women, men, they all feel a desire for wildness and for freedom, and you will benefit from knowing many of them, from knowing as wide a variety as possible.

Do not limit yourself
based on illusory differences.

For when one limits oneself, one limits life, learning, experience, possibility, and joy. All these, they are limited when illusion dictates our choices.

Men, women – these labels do not represent people. The people referred to by these illusory labels represent billions of kinds of strengths and light, as many kinds as there are souls.

At that, the man realized that his scattered papers were now stacked neatly and he no longer wallowed in any mud. The wind too, had diminished. Though the roots and the branches were still in his hand and he inside the well, his hold on those things was lighter and his depth in the well was less than it had been. He was better off now, than he'd been before. He was closer.

The freedom and wildness inside him had grown and the beauty of both caused a smile to creep to his face as he sat then. The creeping smile grew. It grew because he understood now that the wildness and freedom that he sought, was sought by many and not by one group only. It grew too because he understood more, that *all* that he experienced is experienced by all and not one.

His smile in wildness and freedom and peace became the joy of the sun on skin, it became the beauty of the moon and the stars. His God Seed grew inside of him then. The light within it intensified and some of the debris and detritus surrounding it fell away.

His veil lowered for a time, his dissonant motion eased, the man became his smile, his smile became joy and he became all of the things which exist inside of joy – freedom, peace, both wildness and place, orderliness and chaos, plans and spontaneity, connection and oneness. Knowing this, he rose.

He kissed The Woman, seated still, gently upon her head in thanks, and he parted from her, walking.

He called out to her in his growing peace, his thanks without words, as he went.

She knew pleasure that She had been able to contribute a small piece to the eventual permanence of the change in this God Seed.

She would have walked on then, but another man called out to Her from the gathered crowd behind the first man.

But I am a protector, called this man behind. *I seek only to protect those around me. How can* this *be bad?*

The Woman turned toward this voice and saw the God Seed there moving hurriedly, endlessly, legs, arms, mouth, everything – moving without end, without peace. She saw beings around this one, creating other motives that floated his own motive.

Your instinct, The Woman said to this Seed, *toward protection of others is not itself a bad thing.*

It fails,

    It becomes a bad thing,

      when it becomes protection of your loved ones –

From THEMSELVES.

For then, it is oppression.

Do not seek to make those around you better, to force them to live to the standards you desire for them, for then you are only protecting your own self from the work and effort and pain that your own growth would require of you.

Cowardly is the false protection of others from themselves because it is in reality your own lack of bravery for the growth you need to do for yourself.

The God Seed who had spoken did not like this answer. He heaved harder against the roots and branches and even against the people around his pit of fire. He was, in fact, inclined to violence to protect his mind from the Truth of The Woman's words.

But violence never stopped a Truth from being True and so, in time, the Seed found, moving on, that the Truth he despised could not, neither by despising it, nor by railing against it, be made untrue.

All that had happened, all that would continue to happen until the Seed could change himself, was what has always happened since the dawn of time – he left behind himself a path of destruction. In its wake, joy and growth withered and shriveled and distanced themselves from him.

The Woman remained seated, and there She slept and the next morning when night became day, She walked on.

But as She went, outward toward them both and toward the group gathered, She held Her Hand. Though She went on, She was there beside them too. Each would see Her kneeling there, in the flowers, beside him, and always would. Her Hand held out.

Because,

    perhaps,

        one day,

one would want to know the garden,

would want to experience the pathway behind the garden.

Perhaps,

        one day,

            one would seek to experience

The flight, the pain, and the beauty of all of humanity.

*

On and on She walked.

And as She walked, beings came to her: children, animals, seekers, empaths.

One approached Her and fell into step alongside Her. They walked some time like this.

You are an empath, The Woman said then.

Yes.

They walked along a good bit more. Then the man spoke again.

I am also Fatima's father, he said.

Yes, said The Woman. *She walks with you. And, I assume, that means you are also the Colonel.*

It does.

It is always the fighting souls, the soldiers, who see how vain is the fight, isn't it?

In my experience, it is. He paused then and they walked.

I hope to make a bigger change, he said, when speaking again. *One day. My strategic expertise has saved some lives, cost others theirs, but in the end, none of it helps us get at who is right.*

And, in the end, you all stop the fight out of fatigue, not because you have figured out who is right.

And in the fatigue, we haven't figured out the right way forward, the right policy.

You have figured out nothing at all save who has the most money and who can therefore, persevere the longest before the fatigue.

They walked along again then, and when they came to a pond, She sat. Around them water fowl, fish, other birds of many colors went about their lives, as did the children who splashed and laughed beside the water and their parents.

I believe I would better serve, The Colonel said, *by working to create policy. With policy, we can skip over the wasteful, foolish step of fighting the fight that contributes nothing while at the same time creates the next generation of anger and vengeance. It is the never-ending cycle, fighting. It solves nothing, it creates nothing, it teaches us nothing and tells us nothing at all about how to move forward. And it wastes* everything.

The Woman repeated herself. *It is always the fighting souls who see how vain is the fight, isn't it?*

Together they sat. They ate and admired and appreciated all that surrounded them. They sat a while longer yet and felt the air in their lungs, their hearts beating, the oxygen in their blood.

In the morning, the Colonel took his leave of The Woman.

Thank you for your time with me, he said. *I will be touched by the memory of it always.*

Thank you, The Woman said. *The same will be true for*
me. Please, go to the president of your country. Tell him that I
have sent you and that you wish to work on international
policy. He will get you where you need to be to make the
difference you hope to make.

I will, Thank you! I did not know you know our president!

He was perhaps, once upon a time, a simple God Seed in a
well. Many a year ago it might have been that he struggled
more than he does today, twenty years ago and more perhaps.
He yearned to be free then, yet in a deep, deep well of his own
making did he live. I may have been, perhaps, of some little
assistance to him, in helping him to help himself to get closer
to the edge of his well, once upon a time.

Ah, said the Colonel, *I see.* He smiled.

He bowed and walked on then, smiling to himself still.

The Woman, She walked on as well.

But of course, as She went, also She held a Hand. She held
it outward toward the Colonel, that he might know Her
Presence, know She was there for him still...

...and always.

*

On and on She walked.

And as She walked, God Seeds came up to Her: children, animals, seekers, empaths.

Now, many came to Her.

Now, many stayed.

Those who came, now also often gathered loosely around Her.

Even as She moved, so they moved too, the group of them moving as one.

But, said one when they'd been walking some time into the new morning, *are we not instinctive? Are we not herding creatures like the beasts of the field and the insects of the hive?* this God Seed asked of Her.

We are neither herding animals nor social insects though.

Then, are we not like *them?* the God Seed asked, s*imilar, in our desire for the herd and in the instinctiveness of our natures?*

We, have the right, the privilege, to do the work to fully manifest, to become more than instinct, more than chemistry, more than social insects ever building.

And here, beside the river, The Woman stopped, and with Her, stopped the grouping of Seekers, Empaths and God Seeds beside Her.

The Woman, not yet thirsty, had stopped instead in order to say Her morning Thankfulness.

Hands together, eyes closed, She spoke out loud, the words which, most days, were said silently and only to Herself.

Thank you to the sunshine, good morning to the Morning. Thank you for this new day of possibility, opportunity and experiences for everyone.

When She had finished, She paused a moment, still gazing at the wonder of the river. And then She began again to walk.

We *have the right to do the work,* the Woman said, once moving again, as though there had been no pause in movement or words. *We have the right to work to become – fully –* human. *That right is not shared by animals, insects, or even electrons zinging.*

But do we do that?

Is it the fault of possibility, when one chooses not to utilize it?

Well, no, I suppose that it isn't, said the God Seed.

For us, the possibility *to become more exists. It is that which separates us. We can become more.*

It is true, said The Woman as She walked along the edge of the river, *that it is hard to do and that it takes a bit of self-awareness.*

We can *end up as victims of happenstance, the difference is, WE NEED NOT BE.*

We can *end as survivors of what has been done to us, purveyors of what we have been told and have been sold. But, WE NEED NOT BE. Ours is the right to* CHOOSE, *to choose a path of grace and of beauty, to choose to become* human.

The Woman sat beside the water then and lowered Her pack. From it, She removed the items needed for Her small noon day meal. The others did the same.

The insects and the herding beasts, She said then, *they do not have this. We can choose to do the work, to pull ourselves out of the well, to build ourselves of finer material and become men and women – to truly have free will.*

You are right, said the God Seed after a time. *That seems very hard indeed.*

Worry not, for it is not at all nearly so hard as living inside a storm, a fire, or a dark and dank well of unending motion. She finished eating the few bites of the meal She had set out and then She added, *and also, I will be with you.*

The seated God Seeds, pleased and comforted, smiled at this.

And so She walked on then.

But as She went, outward toward them all, She held Her Hand. Though She went on, She was there beside them too. Each would see Her kneeling there, in the flowers, beside him, and always would. Her Hand held out.

Because,

       perhaps,

            one day,

one would want to know the garden,

would want to experience the pathway behind the garden.

Perhaps,

       one day,

            one would seek to experience

The flight, the pain, and the beauty of all of humanity.

*

On and on She walked.

And as She walked, beings came up to her: children, animals, seekers, empaths.

As She walked, a small group appeared in the distance. Over the horizon, one at a time they became visible. She changed not speed nor direction and so eventually the beings came upon Her.

These beings toiled inside Wind and this, they brought with them, along with their churning and disquiet.

She nodded and the troop of Winders fell in beside Her, matching the pace She set.

Before long though, their churning and their volume inside caused, as She had known it would when She nodded, a need in them to speak and in so doing, to rupture the silence with the staccato of their frustration.

Firedwellers, said one, *they carry with them a smell, such a distasteful smell.*

And the Stormers, shouted another, *Such an ignorance they bring! You understand though,* said this being to The Woman, *you are of us, a Winder like us.*

The welldwellers, they could never hope to understand us Winders, chimed in a third. *It is so much better when we spend time amongst just ourselves.*

They went on like this for a time, each encouraging the other in their chatter, each trying to outdo the last.

You must set down your isms, said The Woman then.

She had not waited for a quiet moment, but had spoken curtly into the middle of sentences and bravado, both of which now hung heavy and unfinished on the air. Though no one spoke, there was confusion and murmuring mixed into the disquiet absence of words.

They are too heavy a burden, said The Woman quietly. *Until you set down all your isms, this burden always must you carry.*

The churning increased then. This had been, in the short term, her goal. For She knew that by increasing their dissonance until it became a force that *must* be addressed, a force that could be ignored no longer, it would become a tool for them then, a teacher from which they could begin to learn. The dissonance and churning could not become this teaching tool while it still could be ignored.

That increased dissonance brought increased murmuring with it to the crowd before one at a time, each wandered off, perhaps to think on these thoughts they had heard, or perhaps instead to seek numbing for their dissonance - medications and forgetfulness. She would reach out to them though, with support, for dissonance unsupported is often a dissonance too great.

She noted after a time of walking though, that of these few Winders who had stayed behind and walked along with Her still, there was one who walked filled with questions and longing. The burning in him, for answers, could go undetected only so long after all.

Yes? The Woman said to this Winder. *You wish a path.*

A Stormer approached them then and walked with them. After a time, they were joined as well by several well-dwellers and a fire-dweller.

I want to leave the life I have, and I want to follow you in your teaching, said the Winder God Seed who had not been frightened off elsewhere by Her earlier words.

You are a seeker.

Yes.

But, you are also a parent.

Yes.

Then let your children be your teachers. Allow parenting to be your path.

Parenting...?

Of course.

She paused beside the water they had come upon, and gazing upon beauty, She lifted high the water bottle from her pack before drinking generously of the water. But when She had finished, still he stared blankly, uncomprehendingly, at Her.

Go now, She said. *Let your children remind you of what you already know. Parenting – organically designed and given to provide parents the very development they seek in themselves.*

It is a path... for me?

Organically designed, organically given, yes.

It is not a path through which... I... teach... them?

Of course not, it is a path for your *development. Listen to it. It will remind you daily of where you would like to go, and then, it will help you get there.*

They walked along in a silence then that was for her peaceful and for him, filled with questions.

And isn't it beautiful, She quietly added after a time, *that what creates our opportunity to learn through this nurturing of younger others, is the very act that in itself is the recapitulation of all of human remembrance of beauty – of that higher being that is the union of all things, that is indeed the humanity organism itself.*

He thought on that as he walked, and held his questions in check that he could feel the answers to them inside himself, if he were able.

Others too had approached, many even that the Winders no longer with them had insulted. After the afternoon had passed beautifully into evening and She had sat, the group sitting with

Her, it was one of these, a Well-Dweller, who next sought to break their peaceful silence

But I, I have no children, the Well-Dweller said. *Have I then, no path?*

Do not let the illusion of biology, the inconvenience of it, dictate your family, your children. We all have children. All have family.

For it is in this way only, that we

Nurture The World.

Allow all God Seeds to be your children. And you theirs. That we all learn all that we need, each from the other.

It was the fire-dweller among them who spoke next, his emotions – sadness, fear – unable to be contained any longer.

But one of my *children is very, very sad,* said this God Seed. *So sad, and I know not how to help.*

Yes, said The Woman, *this is a world in which dissonance is commonplace and in which it is both hard at times, to see the good, and at other times, just as hard to feel worthy of it.*

She hoped that they each would see that these concerns were things they shared, all of them, and were not dependent upon the type of struggles each group was focused upon, that it did not depend on whether one's eyes were covered by lenses or veils or soot, these concerns.

Know this though, The Woman began, *that neither maturity nor insight are age-related. Often the young have either greater insight or greater maturity than their parents.*

And so, begin by never holding so tightly to either your erroneous beliefs or immaturity that you cause the dissonance and aloneness in your children to be so great as to be fatal.

Here, The Woman paused. She made a small project of getting an apple and sitting. This She did so that the Fire Dweller could register Her words, perhaps consider them.
After some moments, She began again.

Once, She said, *you have done well with holding less tightly to the wrong things, then*

Stop striving to change your child,
strive instead to change the world.

That is how you can help your child.
But, Precious One, that is no small task that you suggest, said the Fire-Dwelling God Seed, fretful. At his distress, The Woman paused, thinking.
If you have a set of tools, She said then, *and then you swap out one of those tools, or even change one small thing about one of those tools, is not then the entire set changed?*

Well, yes, I suppose that it is.

It is that way with the world. Change just one small thing, a small thing close to you that you can reach perhaps, and you have changed the larger set – the whole world – of which it is a part.

To change the world for a child then requires only that you change one small thing. The Woman paused and sipped the water from Her bottle before continuing. *Perhaps,* She said, *the thing you could start with might be one small something about yourself even. I don't know, perhaps something like, oh, your* perception *perhaps, or your* tolerance *maybe.*

The Woman sat and so the God Seeds walking with Her sat as well.

Then, after your acceptance for things different than you started out expecting has changed, and only then, can you follow that *change up by changing the small bit of the world into which your child wanders – the way in which they are educated for example, or the way they are allowed time and space to learn who they are. Watch them blossom and grow into*

Who They Were Meant To Be

and not who you tell them they must become, and you will know one of the greatest joys that human life can offer any one of us.

The God Seeds of all the different task groups had circled around Her as She spoke. They had, almost inadvertently, crossed their legs on the ground in front of them and placed hands, palm up, upon bent knees. In this way, they sat, they listened. And, perhaps just as inadvertently, they had intermingled themselves. For they were seeing each other (was it for the first time?) as humans. Humans all of them, intermixed, not members of a group, as Us or Them, but just, simply, Humans – Friends, Fellow Travelers, Humans.

After a stretch of peace, The Woman summed up all that She had been trying, to say.

Changing the world to be worthy of the children entrusted in your care, be they biologically connected to you or not, is as easy or as hard then,

As Changing Yourself.

The silence, the stillness, among the God Seeds gathered was beginning to be as complete inside them as it remained outside of them.

.

Please though, The Woman continued, *and this is* SO *important for your child. Be certain,* certain, *to reassure them* *during this time of their youths and their emergence into blossom, for that is a time of great struggle. It is **the** time of greatest struggle indeed.*

Reassure them during this time of struggle, of this, this one solid, unwavering fact –

*that **any** suffering they may cause to you in their growth and struggle,*

Is but a drop of water compared to the ocean of drops that is the joy that they bring!

This reassurance during growth, IT IS CRITICAL. *This next part though is the most important of all, so let me say it twice:*

And then, **GROW** to become a person for whom that is true!

And then, **GROW** to become a person for whom that is true!

The earth continued on its path and day became night and stars became beacons. The stars, they are for us, beacons of joy and of hopefulness in the darkness that would otherwise exist. These beacons twinkled lightly at first and then shone broadly, solidly, brilliantly, consistently, without wavering.

After all of that had happened, after the night had become whole, and the sliver of moon found again the angle of its home in the sky, The Woman, She Spoke again. While She spoke Her few last words of the night to those who'd gathered, a meteor overhead, a shooting star, reminded all who sat of what we beings below truly are, and reminded of what would fall with the death of a star.

The change then, it must come from you.

*

The small troop sat in silence through the night after that, absorbing beauty from the world around them.

As always, that whole night through, some beings came and joined them in their circle, while other beings parted from their company.

Long did they sit, together, in silence.

As daybreak approached, an older God Seed, near the back, spoke up quietly.

It was as if it had taken him much of the day and all of the night, to decide how to put into words *his* pain – a pain of such immensity was it.

I am old though, said this God Seed, and the sadness reverberated from his voice, the pain from out of every cell and fiber of his being.

A*nd I,* he said, *have done much wrong to my children, biological and other, and to many others in the world as well - So very much that is wrong.*

All gathered remained as they'd been – silent and seated – though a tear here or there let the God Seed know that he was not alone in this, his pain.

The silence, peace, and connection all continued forward as the weary man, he shouldered again his burden, attempting once more, to quieten his motion, to find words for his pain.

They will, he began again, *never forgive me should I change now.* He stopped to wipe a tear. *And I do not, I believe, have time enough to change in any case. What then shall become of us, these foolish souls like myself?*

The Woman, to this man, this God Seed, She held out Her Hand.

She stood and went to him, touching him so lightly upon the shoulder.

But more, She reached out to him with Her mind, comforting and offering peace.

He lifted his face to Her and She wiped gently, a tear from his cheek, offering comfort from Her body, spirit and mind before adding with the comfort She would give with Her words.

And then, to him only, this man, to this single God Seed, She spoke.

Time, She said, *is an immeasurable thing. Yet we, you and I, we count it out daily, greedily, hoping to measure that which is immeasurable.*

So, she said, *I will use for you,* your *language of counting. And in that counting, you have at least one day, this day, left*

*to you. You have at least, that much – one day – and in a
single day, so much good can be done. So despair not.*

Yet, The Woman continued after a pause while the sun
rose, *within the space of this thing you call a day, is contained
twenty four of these things you call hours.*

*And, again, within the space of this thing you call an hour,
thirty six hundred smaller units which you call seconds live.*
But,

> *There*

> *The counting stops, because*

> *within the space of the thing you call a second lives not
> one something,*
> *but an infinite, immeasurable number of this thing called,*

MOMENT.

Yes, and still further,

Within each *of the infinite numbers of moments available
within* each *second of time, exists an* infinite *number of
potential futures – things you call*

POSSIBILITIES

In this way, each moment is its own seed,

A Seed of What is Possible.

And in this way, each moment is also

The Seed of What Becomes Possible in the next.

It is looking from this perspective that you see, The Woman continued, *that every single day is not one small thing at all.*

But rather each day is a gift of more than eighty six thousand seconds – and that each of THOSE *is also, not a small gift, not a tiny gift, but is actually,*

an **INFINITE** *gift.*

A gift of Moments,

of Seeds of Possibility,

An infinite gift – of what could become possible.

You call a day one thing, one small slice, one thin, waning, ethereal and fleeting thing, and yet it is actually the most tremendous of gifts –

The gift of eighty six thousand times infinity,

The gift of an infinite number of Seeds of Possibility.

That is what one day is. Nothing is greater or more valuable.

Pick any one of these seeds, on any day, and do the planting and the nurturing to help it manifest, help it grow into what is possible today – that something else will become possible tomorrow.

This I will do! Said the old man whose God Seed still lingered inside his well, or his fire, or his storm. *Thank you, I will do this now.*

But then a shadow moved across the joy of his smile.

But, wisest one, may I ask you one more thing – will they be able ever to forgive me, even were I to plant a seed of possibility?

Forgiveness, my friend, is not the right question. These souls have forgiven you long ago. What they chose to do was to wisely keep their distance and their boundaries, to protect themselves from you until YOU changed.

Change yourself and then make the change real. Only then should you show these others that they can trust in that change – when in fact, they can.

You will learn then, that they forgave you long ago and that what you wanted was shared with what they wanted – that spending time *with you, in addition to forgiving you, would be safe and healthy for them.*

The man's God Seed shown just the tiniest bit brighter then, just the tiniest bit less burdened by the years of debris, and he went off from them with the small start of a song in his heart and perhaps the seeds of a garden in his mind.

The others gathered, they rose and went off too, to be parents, to follow the path, to stop their endless motions, to do what each of them would grow to be capable of doing.

They walked on.

And so, then too, The Woman, She walked on as well.

But as She went, outward toward them all, She held Her Hand. Though She went on, She was there beside these God Seeds too. They would see Her kneeling there, in the flowers, beside them, and always would. Her Hand held out.

Because,

perhaps,

one day,

they would want to know the garden,

would want to experience the pathway behind the garden.

Perhaps,

one day,

they would seek to experience

The flight, the pain, and the beauty of all of humanity.

*

On and on She walked.

And as She walked, God Seeds came up to her: children, animals, seekers, empaths.

On this day though, many came to her – couples these, two by two, they came to her and they were in love. And She could see that in their pleasure and joy, they had inadvertently dropped their branches and roots. One of the two had even stopped working at pushing the endless boulders to and from piles that never varied and never existed.

For a moment, these two even stepped down away from the fires over which they had been burning, slowly rotating and roasting. Two steps further he took, and then another two, because of the momentary courage of love, and when they had each taken two more, they gathered in a deep breath. When slowly it was released again, they remarked on how wonderful, how beautiful was the smell around them, and the flowers, and the birdsong and the world.

Alas, another moment past and all was forgotten again, all the beauty of all the world, and they returned to their fires, their wells, their roots and branches and tasks.

In a moment more, they became consumed and forgot to remind each other of love and of beauty and joy.

But in the space of that moment in time, several days on earth had elapsed and this is what She saw in those days. She saw that on the second day, one was asking of the other why he had been pushing boulders and what had the roots been for him, if he was doing so much more than surviving now, without them? His arms, they felt light to him.

On the fourth of the days within this moment, another noted to Her that, no matter how hard she'd worked, what she'd called progress had taken her farther from understanding, farther from self, and from thriving, and so was not progress but was a devolution. And in that moment they understood, each of them, the false grail that beckoned them.

On the sixth day though, the arms of another of the lovers began calling to the being of whom they were a part. The arms, they felt no longer light, no longer unburdened, but now felt simply empty instead.

We used to hold tight to something, his arms whispered to him. *It was a good and comforting feeling,* they lied to him, *the feeling of holding tight to something.* His legs too, began to whisper We *did* something before – but the piles never varied, The Woman said – and therefore were of *value,* the body continued, ignoring The Woman. The muscles of his body began to clench and unclench.

On the next day, the piles of boulders mocked him.

When the end of their moment found them, each of them, back in place above their fires or their roiling waters or beneath their windstorms, each scrambling for roots and branches, The Woman could hear the whispers.

But She knew, it was the just the habits and their bodies speaking to them.

In the space of the twinkling which is the death of a single star, the clear sight that love's new perspective had brought, was gone again, for the pull of the habits of body and mind are strong, very strong, and are self-reinforcing.

Perhaps one day, they would build themselves of the stronger material, the finer material that will allow them to withstand the pull of habit of body and mind, and to pull themselves out of their wells and fires and to become more than electron, insect or animal, to become *human*.

But that day was not today.

And so She walked on.

But as She went, outward toward them all, She held Her Hand. Though She went on, She was there beside them too. They would see Her kneeling there, in the flowers, beside them, and always would. Her Hand held out.

Because,

       perhaps,

            one day,

they would want to know the garden,

  would want to experience the pathway behind the garden.

Perhaps,

       one day,

            they would seek to experience

  The flight, the pain, and the beauty of all of humanity.

*

On and on She walked.

And as She walked, God Seeds came up to her: children, animals, seekers, empaths.

As She walked, She could see, in the distance, two figures approaching Her.

It was Fatima's father, the Colonel, returning. Beside Fatima's father walked another God Seed.

It was the God Seed of long ago.

Her God Seed.

Hello, Mr. President, said The Woman, and this She said inside Her mind.

Hello, Most Precious One! Said that first God Seed, from inside of his mind.

And so, She smiled. And with Her smile, She paused Her walking.

Toward Her, these other two continued their own walking.

May I? asked that first God Seed when they were still too far for words.

She nodded a slight nod toward the figures approaching.

You may.

When he had arrived in front of Her, the president leaned in and upon Her cheek, he placed the gentlest of kisses. It was a kiss of thanks where words would never do.

You still smell to me of richest loam and most ancient of process, The God Seed said to Her, his smile outshone the sun overhead. *You still remind me, with that smell, of all the beauty of all the world throughout all of time.*

And you, I see, you are kicking oh so very much less these days than in the days of your youth.

Ah, true. Your doing, that.

And now.

And now.

I see. Even still there is that love.

Always.

They stayed together, the three of them, among all who had gathered, throughout the evening and into the next day dawning. All the while, they spoke to each other, sometimes with words, sometimes without.

When the new morn broke, the God Seed had one question remaining, one final request, for The Woman who had been his first and always love.

Tell me, my Precious One, said the president, *more now please, about the organism of which we are all a part, the organism which you can feel, pulsing all around us all.*

You wish for me to speak to you of the record of humanity? Of the humanity organism?

I do, please, I wish it.

Somewhat surprised, She thought on this. Indeed, perhaps it was that now this God Seed who'd struggled so very long inside of his well, perhaps now he would be capable of hearing? The Woman wondered - perhaps. But, She did not know however, in what language, with what words, to begin to express the inexpressible, the ineffable. She thought a while as the sun rose in the sky and She said Her morning thankfulness. She thought while She breathed slowly in, then breathed slowly out, sensing, feeling the breath as it came, as it went. And then, She spoke.

Think, then, She said, *of a grove of aspen trees.* She paused before continuing. *The trees, they appear to you as discreet, individual trees, within a forest of trees, do they not?*

They do.

But, of course, an aspen grove is not separate, individual trees. It is one organism – the whole grove. Such is the same with the mushroom fungus – Armillaria – all one organism, the largest on our planet in fact, save for the Human Organism.

We feel so discrete, so separate from each other, said the God Seed to The Woman.

We feel separated even from ourselves much of the time though, don't we?

I know I do.

And all of society around us is reinforcing this notion of discrete separation that our skin and our bodies suggest to us. But were we to build ourselves of a material strong enough, fine *enough, to feel unseparated from ourselves, we would begin to hear our connectedness, we would smell it and feel it and even see it and recognize in ourselves our place within the human organism and the oneness of all things.*

The God Seed and all the other God Seeds gathered, thought about that for a long space of time. An hour gone, perhaps more, and then he spoke again.

So...then... he began, *when we fight, we...*

Fight ourselves, kill *ourselves.*

Again, for an hour or more, the president and the colonel, sat in silent pondering with the gathered others.

If we could better understand then, he said when he finally spoke again, *that our fights, our wars, are only one part of our own organism fighting another part of our own self.*

The Woman nodded slowly. She waited a respectful space of time – minutes, before speaking further.

Until we build ourselves of that finer material though, gain free will and cognizance as fully human, we cannot recognize ourselves. Until then, until we recognize ourselves, the illusion that

Fraternal islands are we all,

forever to remain just separated brothers,

will remain an illusion we all unknowingly reinforce again and again and again.

The group gathered, stayed gathered after that. The group of them, pondering, stayed pondering, after that.

As afternoon became dusk, it became that time wherein Her God Seed would have to go, to return to his duties, now before a nation.

When the parting was at hand and the two had said their good-byes, their words of a temporary nature, the colonel now interjected.

Then catch up with me, the president told him as he turned and walked away from The Woman and the colonel.

Like this God Seed now parting from us, the colonel said, *Fatima too, has benefitted from her interaction with you.*

She now, I sense, said The Woman, *is in a position that will allow her to use her maturity, her true and developed* Humanity, *in decision making that will bring benefit and joy, for many of the peoples in many of the lands of this world,* The Woman said. *Authority, I sense.*

Indeed, she is. Secretary General now, of the body known to us as, the UN. I will tell her of our visit.

Good. Do, please. She was and always will be, one of my many, many favorites among this, my favorite of species. The Organism needs more like your daughter, The Woman said.

And then the colonel too, leaned in and placed upon the cheek of The Woman, the gentlest of kisses. It too, was a kiss of thanks.

He turned and smiled, and with a wave, he walked on, toward the figure now receding into the distance.

And so, She too walked on.

But as She went, outward toward him, toward them both and all these others, She held Her Hand. Though She went on, She was there beside each of them too. They would see Her kneeling there, in the flowers, beside them, and always would. Her Hand held out.

Because,

perhaps,

one day,

One of them might want to experience

the pathway behind the garden.

Perhaps,

one day,

One would seek to experience

The flight, the pain, and the beauty of all of humanity.

*

On and on She walked.

And She felt, around Her as She went, another, like Herself.

She felt its presence, this other God Seed Made Real, as She walked.

She was moving toward it, this other soul – and it was moving toward Her.

Ahead of this soul She felt, arrived other beings. These beings arrived wrapped in a single, flowing cloth such as might be a uniform of one wishing to be humble, yet She knew, they struggled mightily in their wells and above fire or below storm. This She saw clearly as they moved near Her.

Their words preceded them as well and in their words, She heard many things, but She heard as well, a title. Lama. The Dalai Lama.

Ah, The Woman thought, *the precious one. He is here.*

And the lama could feel presence of The Woman as well and thought to himself, *Ah, the precious one. She is here.*

Behind the uniformed others, came the soul of the one called lama and the two walked until they stood each directly in front of the other, and then they stopped.

And She knew this being and this being knew Her.

There was no pretense in this God Seed, no pretense that this soul did not sense this recognition, no pretense that the communication that occurred between them did not occur, and

Because the pretense of impossibility was absent, the possible transpired with ease.

Mind to mind, without words, without hesitation, their communication transpired.

Instantaneously.

Completely.

The instantaneousness of it did not upend the being called lama, did not unsettle its understanding of time, creating from that fear, the secondary emotion anger.

All of their past lives, all of their future lives, their oneness with the humanity organism and the thing called world, transpired for them together in that moment, that infinite moment, and together they remembered the world as it had been and will be and has always existed. Together they re-lived their births and lives and deaths. They felt each other's thoughts and in those thoughts shared again the experience of being sent together long ago with a small number of others like themselves, they re-lived the experience of getting separated from the others in the immeasurable span that is time and space. Together they went to the garden then they went to the gate at the back of the garden. Because neither pretended the pathway beyond did not exist and because the access, connectedness, to the pathway had not been forgotten or covered over with debris for either of them, they fell together joyfully out upon the pathway beyond and danced and flew, in joy and fulfillment, through all the beauty and all the suffering that had ever been experienced.

Everything that had ever been experienced by anyone, all of it came to them. This they both remembered, and yet were also experiencing for the first time.

Together, dancing, they shared and understood the flight, the pain and the beauty of all of humanity.

It was this that was the cosmos.

This, what they two shared.

And it was this which the physical sharing between other God Seeds, other spouses, is but the tiniest of micro-cosms.

*

Though all of this had taken but a moment, one single Seed of Possibility, She stayed by this God Seed called lama until sunset. Together they shared the experience, the joy, the beauty and fullness that is Two Minds Dancing.

When the last of the rays of the last of the colors had blended into the trees and they were in darkness fully, they parted.

As they parted, She sensed a question - *You wear no uniform.*

And in the same instant, the lama sensed his answer - *Uniform has lost its ability to help us remember humility and in so remembering, be free from ego. Now it is that recognition of the uniform comes to us from God Seeds, thus the uniform has become about ego. I shed mine in my journey, both to be free of ego and to see who does recognize my soul without the clothing to mark it.*

An interesting experiment and journey that, this soul they called Lama said to her without words, *I have often done the same.*

He laughed and She laughed and the laughter was joy-filled and bounced and echoed and volleyed throughout the valley and beyond the trees.

And so, She walked on.

But though their bodies moved in directions different from each other as She walked on, forever would they remain connected. Forever had they worked together in the world, forever would their work together continue, for it was this that was the cosmos, of which all else is only a smaller cosmos, a microcosm.

And so, as She went, and as he also went, outward each toward the other, would they hold a Hand of remembrance. Still.

Always.

*

On and on She walked.

She now found herself on a beach. She had walked to the Atlantic coast.

As She walked, as always, beings came to her: children, animals, seekers, empaths.

The Woman bent and removed Her sandals that She could enjoy the feel of the sand against her skin. She looked to the space where sky and sea met and admired again: One Life, Two Sources.

As She straightened, sandals in hand, a child ran in Her direction from a blanket on the sand behind The Woman. It was a happy, laughing, smiling child who might have been running toward the water, except that The Woman knew that the child was not.

Momma, called out the child, opening its arms to The Woman.

The Woman turned from the water and toward the sand and swept the child up at the last moment that the toddler would not be swept away into the roaring ocean.

She did this sweeping up with such joy that it became both the cause and the effect of Her newest understanding. She understood that She had fallen in love.

She had sought a single human, but instead had found Herself in love with the whole of the Humanity Organism; a species so deep inside of their own wells as to be very nearly unlovable, this organism and yet foolishly, joyously, in love with the whole of it, The Woman now found Herself.

I am not your momma, The Woman said to the child, *but I am* The *Momma.* She kissed the head of the child and set her down again on the sand.

But the child cried out to be again lifted by The Woman. A nod from the tall man approaching behind the child and The Woman bent again and lifted the child a second time. The child laughed at that and cried out happily over the head of The Woman allowing herself to fall back from The Woman, arms open wide as if attempting to utterly and completely embody all that is joy itself. Toward the sea the child clapped, her laughter sailing out far in front of her.

She is so happy with you, the tall man, now approached, said.

Happier than hoarded fresh berries in the byre, I hope.

The man had been watching his happy grandchild but now his head and attention focused sharply upon The Woman. He was silent for a time and then spoke quietly.

You know Seamus.

Or he knows Me, and in the end it is the same.

It was in the moment of his non-response that She felt the wave of knowledge that rolled off of him. This one, he was capable, would be capable with Her, of Two Minds Dancing.

She smiled then, mostly to Herself, and She took his hand.

Without a word, they turned and walked along in the sand, the child between them.

They walked in silence for a stretch of time and then too, they spoke at length as the child played.

The child turned then, to run up away from the water toward her parents.

Grandma would have liked this lady, Grampa, she said and the man's breath caught at that, before a smile came to his face and he nodded to the child. The child smiled at The Woman and waved happily, and then she turned away and ran to her waiting parents.

Motion had been valuable, when She had begun, as a means of keeping desperate souls from swamping Her in their desperation. But, She had met several souls now, who were fully unlike the others. And she had met many more on her travels, who had, at least, *begun* their evolution – and so were, in this way, at the beginning of the process of becoming fully and truly Human.

This was enough, the few She'd met. It was, for Her simple needs, sufficient.

And because it was sufficient, these few She had met, Her long walk, She knew, was now done.

The moment of quiet which befell them at the girl's departure was one of peaceful, easy exchange between them and they, as one, turned and resumed what was now only a stroll.

Yours is not, you know, the typical response I usually cause in people, the tall man said to The Woman then.

Nor yours mine, The Woman chuckled.

But then The Woman paused a moment and seeing his seriousness, She looked up into the sun. She shielded her eyes with her hand and then returned Her eyes to the sand as they walked along a bit further.

If you are referring to your celebrity, She said, and here the woman looked up at him again, *I am aware of it.* She paused and shielded again Her eyes. *I am simply more interested in your humanity.*

At this, the man paused his motion and turned toward The Woman, a tear coming to his eye. He stayed like that for many moments. Then he smiled and gently took up The Woman's hand in his own again.

Many minutes passed before he spoke.

Of course you are, he said then, *how could it have been any other way?*

*

The two walked together like that, helping others to remember, through the remaining years of their lives in these bodies. The Woman helped some through Her connection with The Dalai Lama, others with Her time spent in the hospitals, still others by simply being still. She did this because what else would a God Seed Made Real do with the rest of Her days on Earth but gently reach out to those souls nearest Her and to do so in ripples – circular waves in size ever growing?

It was that, all their years of sharing, comforting, guiding and simply *reminding*, which had been made possible in that single moment when She had looked up at the grandfather and spoken.

For what else is a single moment but a single Seed of Possibility within millions, each one a seed of what becomes possible in the next?